THE BASEMENT DWELLERS

DAVID LOPERA

www.davidloperafiction.com

Cover art by Sandeep Karunakaran (Sanskarans).

www.instagram.com/sanskaransart

www.artstation.com/sanskarans

www.facebook.com/Sanskarans

"The path to paradise begins in hell."

-Dante Alighieri

PROLOGUE

"COLETTE!" Charles Dupré called from the library at the back of the house. "Colette, come here! I'd like to read you a story."

Charles, sporting a smoking jacket, sat in his comfortable French Napoleon armchair with an old leather book in hand. Colette rushed into the library, running past tall shelves packed with leather-bound volumes, her frilly dress fluttering behind her. Her red ringlets bounced as she leapt onto her father's lap, her expression excited.

"Whatcha fixin' to read to me tonight, Pa?"

Colette, only six years old, giggled and leaned against his broad chest, her eyes on the book in his hand.

"It's an ol' tale from ancient Egypt called The Boat of Millions of Years, sugarplum. Reckon you'll take a shine to it."

Colette nodded, eyes bright. "O-oooh! Now that's a purty name for a tale! It sounds like a real good'un!"

Dupré pivoted his daughter on his lap so she faced the

leatherbound book, his eyes drifting to the dark beyond the almost closed curtains.

"Read, read!" she said, her fists pumping.

Mr. Dupré opened the book and began to read.

"Long, long ago, thousands upon thousands of years ago, back in the time of ancient Egypt, there was a magical boat that glistened with the colors of purple amethyst, green emerald, jasper, turquoise and bright blue lapis lazuli. It shone with the lustre of gold. The Egyptians called this boat Mandjet... The boat of a million years."

"Why did they call it the boat o' million years, Pa?" Colette asked, tilting her head to look up at him.

"That's a mighty fine question, sugarplum," Charles said. "I'll answer every last one of 'em after the tale is done. You reckon you wait?"

Colette nodded. "Yes, Pa."

"This magical boat sailed through the beautiful sky all the way from the East to the far West bringing light and heat to shine down on all the world. Every morning, the sun god of the ancient Egyptians opened the doors of the sky and boarded this boat. He sailed high up into the heavens and filled the land and the people with life-giving sunlight. But at the end of each day, as the sky grew dark and sullen, the Egyptians looked up and wondered, 'Where does the sun go at night?' Just as the sun god traveled the bright sky in the day, the night spirits continued his journey during the night. Every evening, the night boat and the gods who navigated it took a dangerous journey. They sailed deep into the murky territory of the Duat, the ancient Egyptian underworld, dark with night and full of the unknown..."

Colette shivered in his lap, snuggling closer. "Pa, this tale here's kinda scary."

"It's almost done. Do you want me to stop?" Charles

closed the book, leaving his finger as a placeholder, tightening his arms around her.

"No, no!" She pushed away, sitting straighter. "Keep goin'."

"All right, then..." He opened the book again and carried on:

"Here, just like within the great River Nile, crocodiles, snakes and all kinds of dangerous and powerful creatures lurked within the shadowy water. One enormous and dangerous snake, the serpent Apep, swam beneath the boat and thundered his terrifying roar. The sound made the whole underworld shake. Every night, Apep followed the boat, its mouth wide, trying to swallow the boat and everyone within. He wanted to stop the sun from rising in the morning. He wanted to stop the light. But every single night, the boat and its crew prevailed. Using spears, they fought off the enemy snake and threw off the cover of darkness, and they sailed off towards a bright new day. And so it was that, each and every morning, the sun god would reappear, victorious, in the East of the horizon."

He closed the book and looked down at Colette, safe in his arms, her bright curls crushed against his chest. She yawned, stretching as he finished. It was well past her bedtime.

"Well, now, whatcha think about that?" he asked.

She smiled up at him, her eyelids drooping. "Ah liked it! It was a little scary, but Ah'm glad the sun god came back. Ah cain't imagine having to live without the sun."

Charles tousled her hair and kissed her on her forehead.

Anne Dupré, Colette's mother, came in from the hall, her dark red hair unbound against her white cotton nightdress.

"I think it's time for you to get ready for bed, missy.

Come along now," Anne said, kissing her husband's cheek before she ushered her daughter out of the library.

Left alone, Charles poured himself a glass of cognac and lit a cigar. He picked up the book he'd been reading to Colette, stared at it for a long moment, and muttered to himself: "the sun god."

PART ONE

OPEN YOUR MOUTH

LOCATION: UNKNOWN – 2004

CASIMIR JAWORSKI FELT THICK, his boney arms and limbs melting into the saggy pit of quicksand he knew as a couch. He struggled to push to his feet, fighting against gravity while the heavy metal music rattled his brain. Something was terribly wrong.

Am I going to die? Or, am I already dead? Cas thought.

The music's distorted guitar and heavy drums kicked at his temporal lobe. His heart pounded. Across the room, a fuzzy television set transmitted a Formula One Grand Prix race, the screams from the cars' engines rumbling as they raced past the cameras.

"Could you turn down the music? Please! Turn it down!" Cas bawled, attempting to project his voice over the analog speakers. A tangle of messy wires made it difficult to navigate the basement floor and his head felt like a train veering off its rails—his brain sliding against his cranium.

She gave me too much, he thought to himself. *Why'd she give me so goddamn much?*

Jazzie, Casimir's friend and crush, had kept giving him Nex. When he asked Jazzie if it contained any heroin, meth, or cocaine, she swore to him it didn't.

Cas remembered the first time he'd tried the stuff. Initially, during that first trial run, his hands and fingers tingled. Now, his skin felt like it was melting off his bones. The intensity of the hallucinogenic concoction (or whatever it was) was impossible to describe with words; with any form of linguistics.

Seth, Jazzie's older brother, stumbled over to the stereo and forced the dial hard right. The music blared at ear-piercing levels, the decibels overkill. Seth bared his teeth at Cas, gaze fiendish.

Jazzie snuck up behind Cas. He spotted her lush, reddish-gray hair from his periphery. Cas never understood why a girl as young as Jazzie had so much fine gray hair tangled among her vibrant reds. He wondered if it was a genetic trait or if she had it styled and colored that way. He'd never had the courage to ever ask her about it. He'd only met Jazzie and her brother Seth the summer before. He knew some things about his friends, but Seth and Jazzie, for the most part, were still a mystery.

"Open your mouth," Jazzie purred. Cas did as he was told without protest. He did so because he would've done anything Jazzie asked of him. He would have jumped off the Brooklyn Bridge or the Empire State building, or any other New York City landmark for that matter, if she'd asked him to. She put a syringe up to his lips and pressed the plunger, squirting scarlet liquid into his mouth. The metallic bite of Nex cut into his soul. Nex wore the veil of holiness. The drug was a demon's disguise, a shadowy devil, only to reveal himself once the user's inhibitions were down. The lights began to dim and everything turned carbon black.

Seth and his sister, Jazzie, hosted most drug-induced extracurricular evenings at their house on Fridays and Saturdays. They only hung out in their basement, which they entered through the basement hatch around the back of the house. Cas had been to their house over a dozen times but he'd never been upstairs. Their basement was like a secret hideout where they could do whatever they wanted, since Seth and Jazzie's dad never came down to bother them.

Most nights were a blur of drinking games, PlayStation, or simply watching humdrum reality TV shows or reruns of sitcoms. Tonight, Casimir's mind ripped open; logic struggled to hold its ground as a tidal wave of primeval thoughts flooded him.

"Are you the devil?" Cas hoped he'd said the words out loud, his skin burning hot, then freezing cold.

Mocking laughter assaulted his senses.

He wasn't sure who or what was laughing at him. It didn't sound human. The bright blue walls pulsated, laughing maliciously, as they cramped in on his thin frame. *Am I still in the same basement?*

His chest tightened, ribs squeezing. The change in his breathing made him feel vulnerable. And lost. He wanted it to end, but his dread grew as he realized this was only the beginning.

Everything around him seemed to liquefy, resembling a Dali painting he'd seen once at the Guggenheim Museum. Images of an ancient person casting glass seared his sight. Visions of a primitive tradition—either Ancient Egyptian or

Mesopotamian—flashed through his cortex, red and scalding. Something smelled foul, like meat decaying for far too long.

Cas looked around for something to anchor him, bring him back to the present. The room kept shifting, his legs wobbling to maintain his balance. Until he saw something dark and stable to his right.

Seth sat on his cathedra—a chair with a high perch he'd picked up on the curb of a wealthy neighborhood. Cas had helped Seth pick up the chair last winter. It fit perfectly in their hangout, where most of the furniture was either picked from the street or found at yard sales, a hodgepodge of knickknacks and haphazard styles. It didn't matter. They were teenagers and they didn't have much money. *At least they had a place to hang out and do drugs*, Cas thought.

Cas closed his eyes for a moment, a red flush rising up his cheeks as he clenched his fists. *What was in that stuff they gave me? What if it kills me?* He'd hung out with them dozens of times and considered them close friends. So why did he feel like they'd betrayed him? *Furtive emissaries from hell.*

Something was definitely wrong.

Seth's chair, along with his tyrannical glare, made him look like Ramses—the great Egyptian Pharoah ruler who ruled through torment and torture. It felt like his dark eyes pierced Cas' soul, leaving him frozen in time.

Move! His body wouldn't obey.

Why can't I move? Casimir thought. *What kind of drug is this?* Wonder turned to fear and fear turned to panic.

"I know you'd like to leave, Casimir. Unfortunately, that won't be happening," Seth bellowed, his voice full of disdain. The words knocked and reverberated against the walls.

"...won't be happening... be happening...appening... ening...ing...ng..." They echoed on and on and on in Cas' mind. Space and time, along with all of the atoms and all matter in the Universe, stretched on. The cosmos averted its gaze from Casimir, remaining silent, indifferent, to the suffering the teenage boy was experiencing.

Here I am, about to die, at seventeen.

He'd argue with his mother—have philosophical debates —regarding the existence of God, though he really had no firm belief in anything. He figured he was agnostic but, on this evening, his views began to alter.

Despite his confused religious beliefs, he prayed. *Saint Casimir, if you are real, if you can hear me, please help me get out of this mess.* His helpless feeling didn't waver. *I'm a contradiction,* he thought. *One second, I think there's no such thing as God. Next, I'm praying for help. I'm a fraud and I'm probably going to die in this basement. Or, wherever the hell I am.*

Why am I praying? Agnostics don't pray, Cas thought. He wanted to laugh at his own ridiculous introspections, but saw no humor in his situation. And the heat grew around him, hot whispers across his skin.

The walls morphed, origami-like, into a regal throne room that resembled an immense chamber from an Egyptian castle. The distance from one wall to another expanded every time Cas blinked. The granite and stone reminded him of images he'd seen in his world history text-book. Hieroglyphics, signs, and ciphers—Ankhs, Djeds, scarabs, Eyes of Horus—enveloped the high walls, propped up by lotus columns.

Seth now wore a shendyt—a short kilt-like garment. Distant cries and moans could be heard through the shifting walls, and Cas' heartbeat accelerated, sweat making him clammy and hot at the same time.

"Am I in hell?" Cas breathed the words out, sure he didn't want the answer. *Perhaps a mortuary temple?* The shifting surroundings and a feeling in the pit of his aching stomach, propelled Casimir to think he was, all of a sudden, somewhere else—somewhere *unknown*.

His mind attempted to recall how he'd gotten there. He struggled to remember, trying to sort through his thoughts and memories like a person using a sieve, desperate to catch something of value.

He was responsible somehow, but he couldn't remember how or why. The drug had eviscerated his memory. He felt intense guilt. Heavy guilt that made him feel as if an anchor had ensnared his chest and was pulling him down and down into a black water abyss.

Seth's hair had grown into a long blond mane, and he held Cas' gaze with a stare of pure evil. *The devil incarnate,* Cas thought. He tried to avert his gaze and began to tremble violently.

Seth had fangs.

I'm imagining this, he thought. *Not real.*

Cas looked again, just one second. Seth's fangs grew longer, ivory white, piercing the sides of his mouth, drops of blood running down his jaw to pool in the hollow of his throat.

Cas choked under ash, cinder and burning stone. *Was I sent to one of Dante's Bolgias?* Cas considered which circle of hell he'd been sent to. Maybe the eighth circle—the one reserved for fraudsters.

I'm not leaving this barbarous pit, Cas admitted to himself, resignation seizing hold of his spirit. His mind raced to think of an escape route. He attempted to get up, but realized he was already standing, his mind a scattered jigsaw puzzle.

Jazzie's lips were kissing his ear. "Try to enjoy it," she said softly. "It hurts when you fight it."

Am I going to die? Am I already dead? The existential question repeated in his mind. Cas was unable to speak or yell, and grim notions fluttered through his mind. He wanted to shout *help*, but couldn't move his mouth to form the word.

A jarring growl rumbled from Jazzie's throat, tickling his ear, and Cas saw Jazzie had fangs just as terrifying as her brother's.

Vampires! How did I get mixed up in this shit? Fuck me! Cas couldn't move, couldn't see a way out, hated he'd fallen for this. Doomed.

Jazzie's fangs sank deep into Cas' neck, her lips cold and firm against his tender skin. As Jazzie drained blood from Cas' neck, any sound he made disappeared into the booming music, his vision engulfed by the blackness of waning consciousness.

CHAPTER 2
NAWLINS

QUEENS SHIMMERED in a haze of smog and exhaust fumes in the late afternoon heat. A suffocating blanket of dense air clung to Andrew Byrne's exposed pores. He'd decided to throw a kegger—a soiree where underage teenagers managed to acquire a good amount of beer—and the oppressive humidity wasn't going to stop him, or his friends. Keggers were a special affair for high schoolers. Andrew and his buddies had their connections, usually an older friend or someone with a foolproof fake ID. Today, two kegs were being delivered to his house in the back of a 1992 Nissan Altima. How one had fit in the backseat and another in the trunk of that Altima was a wonder no one could fathom, but somehow, they'd fit.

Andrew and his classmates were a few weeks away from summer vacation, close to wrapping up their junior year of high school and it felt like the proper occasion to celebrate.

Casimir and Andrew strode out the front door once they'd gotten word the kegs had arrived.

"Another year in the books, boys," Andrew said, as he, Casimir, and two of their friends lugged the keg out of the trunk. He used his father's hand truck to wheel them around the house through the backyard to minimize the chances of nosey neighbors spying on them taking delivery of alcohol. The tall hedges surrounding the sides and back of the house assisted them with their ploy.

"We need some muscle here," Andrew said, as they lifted the one hundred sixty-pound keg up the back steps and moved it into the kitchen.

"Careful, dude," he said, as they scraped across his mother's spotless tile kitchen floor. His parents were away at their summer house, and they'd murder him if they found out he'd thrown a party at their home. He was already making mental notes of how much clean-up he'd have to do before they returned.

At about a quarter to nine, as if summoned by magic, teenagers appeared on Andrew's front steps in droves. Some were friends and acquaintances from St. Thomas Aquinas Catholic Preparatory—the high school Casimir and Andrew attended. But most flowed from other schools —public schools around Queens. Some were high school dropouts from unknown origins and backgrounds, looking to prey on young, naive girls as they imbibed alcohol and marijuana in communion. Most, if not all, of the party's guests were already drunk on cheap whiskey and beer and excessive amounts of cannabis (and Lord knows what other illicit substances) by the time they arrived.

Andrew's family home, a Dutch colonial with prim boxwood-framed walkways and a cozy backyard, hadn't been christened by a high school party until that evening. His parents took great care of the house. The front lawn was meticulously trimmed, shrubs pruned, plants alive and verdant that summer. Andrew's dad sometimes mowed the lawn but, for the most part, his parents hired landscapers to keep it picture perfect.

Inside the house, the walls were a soft white with nice framed prints and family portraits hung at regular intervals. In the dining room, a China cabinet housed antique plates, glasses, and other Byrne heirlooms passed down in their family for decades. The dining room table was large enough to seat twelve people comfortably. It was a home filled with lovely decor and gentle touches put together with hard work and grinding sweat. His parents' pride and joy. Andrew looked at the crowd of teenagers and had his first moment of doubt.

Once word had gotten around, by ten o'clock that Saturday night, his house was bouncing with over one hundred and twenty young partygoers, and an estimated ninety of them, give or take, hadn't been on the proverbial *list*. Andrew raced from the living room to the dining room, where Veronica, a brunette Latina who also attended St. Thomas Prep, had rolled a Bob Marley-like spliff, ten inches long, as thick as a tiki torch. She pulled out a lighter from a slouchy bag she had strung around her chest and lit the sucker up. Gray fumes filled the living room air in a matter of minutes.

"No smoking weed inside the house," Andrew said, trying his best to sound authoritative. He'd been huffing and puffing all night, shuffling from one room to another, pleading with his guests, but his words landed on deaf ears. "Come on, smoke that outside!"

He was out of breath trying to put out fires, literally. A boy he didn't recognize rested a cigarette on his dining room table, a centimeter away from setting the table cloth and the entire table ablaze. Another delinquent had flung a massive

Ziploc bag full of marijuana on the dining table (one pound's worth?). The bag had been left open at the top and the herculean buds spilled out across the surface of the table.

"Please, don't smoke that inside! You can go outside! Go out back!" Andrew begged, his hands clutching fistfuls of his dark hair. His pleas faltered as despair took over his spirit. His parents would be home in two days, and he'd probably have to spend the whole time cleaning up the mess growing around him.

———

Casimir shadowed Andrew from room to room, taking in the depravities unfolding. It was only a quarter past ten, and the regret Andrew wore on his face showed Cas his friend wished he could turn back time and reverse his decision to host the affair at his home. Cas knew it was Andrew's attempt to be seen as the cool guy for once, but the consequences wouldn't be worth the backlash he'd experience when his parents returned home.

The door to the basement was locked. Casimir heard sex sounds—guttural gasps and a cacophony of high- and low-pitched sounds—emanating through the door. He turned Andrew around and steered him away from that door, hoping his friend hadn't heard the moans.

I can't let him go upstairs, Cas thought. All of the bedroom doors were locked and Cas had seen four people enter Andrew's parents' master bedroom. *If Andrew finds out.* The party had to be contained to the main floor; the upstairs bedrooms, especially Andrew's parents' bedroom, were off-limits. Andrew would completely freak out and have a meltdown if he knew strangers were hooking up there.

"Let's go back this way," Cas said, trying to sound nonchalant.

In the dining room, Veronica had the spliff between her lips, already fired up. She exhaled a thick stream of gray smoke, adding to the cloud hanging over the table. Another boy lit his blunt and several people smoked cigarettes in the dining room. Pure chaos, thought Cas.

"I'm fucked," Andrew said. "I'm completely fucked."

"It'll be all right, man. Try to enjoy yourself. I'll help you clean up in the morning," Casimir said blithely, knowing he wouldn't be doing any cleaning but wanting to help his friend relax.

"Why won't people go outside to smoke?" Andrew's voice went up with each word. "How am I going to get the marijuana and cigarette smell out before my parents get back from PA?" Andrew looked frantic, his brown eyes wide with a deer-in-the-headlights look.

Cas scanned the area. It would be nearly impossible to get the smell of smoke out of the house within thirty hours, which was about when Andrew's parents were due to return from their vacation home. He figured Andrew had really painted himself in a corner. But, what could he do now? The party must go on.

Andrew was Casimir's closest friend. The term *best* friend was never used, but they were tight. Cas thought the most appropriate thing he could do to comfort his pal in that moment was to lie to him. A white lie.

"You're going to have to use a lot of Febreze. Don't worry about it right now; we'll get the smell out. I know a few tricks for that," Cas said, surveying the ongoing damage.

But the party was only getting started. "It'll be okay,

man," Cas reassured. The reality was they'd need one of those high-powered filtering systems casinos used to get the heavy smoke odor out, which they obviously didn't have. By ten thirty that night, Andrew's entire house had morphed into an X-rated funhouse.

I need a goddamn beer, Cas thought.

Casimir strolled into the kitchen where the keg had been stationed and noticed, immediately upon entering, a girl he'd never seen before. Her skin was very pale and speckled with tan freckles. Fine copper-gray hair hung past her shoulders loosely, slightly tousled, but not too messy. She wore a black lace cami tank and torn and tattered black jeans in that fashionable, chic way punk and goth kids bought them. A gold necklace with a locket dangled around her neck. Sharp dagger earrings pierced both her ears.

Is there a Marilyn Manson concert tonight?

Cas wasn't a huge fan of goth, but this girl totally pulled it off. A cigarette dangled between her fingers, their blood-red nails matching the lipstick smeared on her lips.

Different from the girls who attended his Catholic high school, that was for sure. She was talking to a lanky girl Cas recognized from St. Thomas Prep, but whose name he could never remember, despite his best efforts. They didn't hang in the same circles and, even though he knew he wasn't exactly Mr. Popular, this other girl was a tiny blip on his radar.

The pale girl, on the other hand, held him with her gaze as she continued talking. "My family is originally from France, so my ancestry is technically French Creole," she proclaimed, taking a drag off her cigarette. The other girl nodded, but said nothing. After making a pretty smoke ring, the pale girl went on, "We have some French nobility in our blood-line, too."

Who's she think she is, Marie Antoinette, for chrissakes?

Cas knew a girl who carried herself like a queen would never be interested in him. She looked like she'd been born into privilege, and most girls he'd encountered with affluent upbringings usually turned their noses up at him.

"Really?" the lanky girl replied, looking vaguely interested.

Cas walked over towards the keg, returning his attention and concentration to his mission: refilling his cup with beer. As he lifted the hose, he stared at the pale girl, now just a breath away from her. They locked eyes. She looked like she needed more iron in her system, Cas decided but, besides that, he was drawn to her mysterious allure.

She ran her fingers through her odd-colored hair, making him wonder whether she'd deliberately added gray streaks to the dark red strands. Her hazel eyes held him mid-motion, his beer cup loose in his grip. She had an aura of danger, almost hunger, like a lion better viewed from the other side of safety glass or a metal cage.

"You're not going to say hello?" She lifted one corner of her mouth in a slight smile, her eyes running from his face down to his feet and back so quickly he wondered if he'd imagined it.

Is she talking to me?

Cas turned his head and looked around at the small semicircle of partygoers hovering near the keg, then realized she had been addressing him.

A small giggle escaped her. "Yes, you, silly."

"He...Hello." Cas stumbled over the word. *Are you ever going to learn to talk to girls? This is exactly why you're still a virgin!* His inner voice, never his greatest fan, yelled at him.

"I'm Jazzie. Nice to meet you." She extended her hand. Cas stared at it for several seconds, too stoned to be talking to a girl he didn't know, especially a girl clearly out of his league.

The lanky girl laughed, breaking the moment of silence. "Way to be awkward, dude," she chimed in.

Yeah, way to be awkward is right, he thought.

Cas clasped Jazzie's slender hand and shook it. Her cold and powerful grip made his heart flutter.

Strong handshake.

He cleared his throat. "I'm Casimir."

"Cassssimeeeer." She repeated his name, taking her time to pronounce the syllables carefully, drawing out the s. She slithered close to him, crinkling her nose.

Did she just smell me? What the—?

"It's Polish," he said. *Why the hell had he said that?*

"Oh, yeah?

"I'm named after a saint," Casimir mumbled, wondering why this stupid stuff was coming out of his mouth.

"Your family must be very religious." Her eyes were half-closed and it appeared to Cas, God help him if he were going mad, that she'd taken another whiff of him. She looked to be relishing the scent of a dessert just out of the oven. Only there wasn't any food around. Just poor little old Casimir.

Okay, either I'm imagining it or she's sniffing me!

He shrugged. "I guess."

Another boy who shared a striking resemblance with the girl (perhaps a sibling or relative?) hovered nearby. He stood aloof and appeared to have been studying Cas, from a few feet away. Cas wasn't sure if the marijuana he'd smoked had increased his paranoia or if this stranger had, in fact, been keeping watch on him. First, he thought Jazzie (what an interesting, but strange, name) had been smelling him. Now, he felt this other fellow was spying on him like a deep cover agent. It was always a coin toss how paranoid he'd feel after he'd smoked reefer. His paranoia meter was redlining hard.

"This is my brother, Seth," Jazzie said, pulling his observer closer towards her—closer to them.

Cas smiled, relieved. *Maybe her brother was being protective. I'm glad they're related and not a couple. She's cute. Strange but cute... Actually, not cute. Jazzie's beautiful.*

The lanky girl snapped the hose away from Cas and inserted herself back in their conversation as she began to fill her cup. "I thought you two were dating," she said, her voice grating, then let out an awkward, high-pitched laugh.

"Sethie?" Jazzie asked, letting out a short cackle. "He's my brother! Can't you tell?" Jazzie tousled Seth's hair, lighter than hers and without the gray streaks that made hers so distinctive.

"Who's older?" The lanky girl asked.

Cas looked at Jazzie, then back to the annoying girl, not sure what to do or say.

Should I get out of here now? Cas felt awkward and didn't see the point of standing around, not adding anything to the conversation. He felt incredibly shy around people he didn't know too well.

"Want to guess?" Jazzie asked, playfully. She peered into Cas' cup and, seeing it was empty, took the nozzle back from the awkward girl and refilled his cup with beer.

"Hmm..." the girl took a long discerning look at the both of them. Her dull brown eyes moved from Jazzie to Seth, and then back to Jazzie.

"I think Seth is older," she finally blurted, still looking back and forth between them, a small frown between her overplucked brows.

"You're correct!" Jazzie clapped her hands, nodding. "Seth is fourteen months older than me. Our poor mother got knocked up back-to-back." She turned and smiled at Cas in a way that made his skin dimple up. It was a statue's smile, no real warmth in it, reminding Cas of her cold grip. She finished filling up his beer and handed it to him.

"Thanks." He took a sip to show his appreciation. "What school do you go to?" Cas asked.

What? You're actually talking to girls now? Bravo, you brave son of a bitch! A rush of bravado filled his spirit. Somehow, almost as if through divine intervention, Cas carried on a conversation with a beautiful girl, as if he were on autopilot and didn't have any control over his actions. There was something inherently magnetic about Jazzie. He felt as if he <u>had</u> to talk to her—a compelling force he couldn't place his finger on.

Have I seen her before? Somewhere?

"So... uh, what school do you go to?" he asked her again.

"School?" Jazzie scoffed, lifting a languid hand. "My brother and I just moved here. We haven't had the opportunity to enroll in a school yet." She looked over in Seth's direction.

Seth nodded. He extended his pale, graceful hand towards Cas.

"I'm Seth, bro. Pleasure to meet you."

A cool breeze fluttered past and caressed Cas' face as their hands clasped together. Seth's gold rings pressed hard against his hand, the flesh around it stiff and chilly. *Cold hands,* he thought. *Just like his sister's. Especially for such a humid summer night.*

"Casimir," he said, inclining his head. "Pleasure to meet you, too. Where'd you move from?"

"Nawlins," Jazzie said brightly.

A young man who'd been refilling his cup with beer, spun around and cut in excitedly: "Yo, you from Nawlins?" he asked with a wide smile. His blue eyes were bloodshot and the smell of marijuana oozed from his pores and clothing.

Jazzie lifted her chin. "That's right," she answered proudly.

"They got dat crawfish, dem po boy sandwiches, dat gumbo down der! I got a aunt who live down der." The boy lifted his beer in salute, slopping some onto the floor.

"Ohhh, do you? Ain't that lovely!" Jazzie replied, her tone uninterested.

"I don't really know too much about Nawlins," Cas admitted. "But it sounds pretty dope."

"It's fire down der!" the boy said, then turned and left the kitchen with a few other strangers.

"Oh, yes! New Or-leens is definitely fire...Down there!" Jazzie let out a high-pitched laugh, almost like a squeal.

Cas smiled, finding Jazzie's shrill laughter endearing.

"The food there is mighty fine, sinful even. You ain't never had no Louisiana cookin'?" she asked, turning back towards Cas. "Ya know about New Orleans, though, right?" She raised her brow. Before he could answer, she kept on, "It's kinda like New York, but a lot more quaint. Another city that doesn't sleep."

Her whole face lit up, and Cas was mesmerized by the change in her. "Got a whole heap o' history, too, an' lots o' Caribbean, French, African and European influences. There's so much history there—from Voodoo to all its haunted past..." Her mouth wouldn't stop moving, as if she hadn't talked to anybody in years. She continued, "Me and my brother, that's where we grew up. You oughta try to visit sometime, Casimir."

"I..." Cas began.

"What school do *you* go to?" Jazzie interrupted.

"Saint Thomas. Most people I know at this party go there, too."

She nodded. "Oh! That's supposed to be a really good school, right? Hear a lot of smarties go there and they have a great athletics program, too." She turned to her brother. "Maybe we can find out about enrolling there, huh, Seth?"

Seth scoffed at his sister. "That's a Catholic school, ain't it? You have to go to mass and pray all the time, right?" Seth asked.

Cas remained quiet, not bothering to tell the other boy he didn't pray all that much, even if he did have to go to mass more than he liked.

"Crosses hung up all 'round the building? Yeah, ain't happenin'," Seth said, then took a sip from his cup. His gaze settled on his sister, a frown darkening his face.

"It's a pretty good school." Cas felt his shyness creeping up on him again. Most of the people he knew—most of his family—were Catholic. He'd met some Pentecostals—family friends and acquaintances—but where he grew up, nearly everyone he knew was Catholic and a small minority were Jewish.

Mormons would knock on his apartment door once or twice a year in an effort to encourage him and his neighbors into joining their camp, offering their free bibles, but his mother would turn them away with a pleasant smile. There was also the one Jehovah's Witness family he knew, but they were outliers.

Was Jazzie not familiar with the term 'saint'? Something told Cas they knew Saint Thomas was a Catholic school and they may just have been toying with him. But why bother?

"Mass?" Jazzie asked, disappointment coloring her expression. "It's been a while since I've been. Maybe not," she said, her voice soft. Her uppity demeanor from a few moments ago wilted like a dying flower. Now, her face was etched with sorrow at the mere mention of mass and crosses.

Seth's face was flat, without any emotion to spare. His pale blue eyes seemed to look right through Casimir as if his thoughts were elsewhere, in some faraway dream.

There's something old and sad about these two, Cas thought. He felt as if he were intruding on a private, painful memory. *Old souls.* He'd heard the term, but it made sense to him now.

Unsure why Jazzie and her brother had such a strong aversion to Catholicism and its Christian symbols, he figured they practiced a different religion, but he didn't want to seem rude or ignorant and ask them about it. *Maybe they're in a cult.*

He'd arrived at a dead end in their conversation. The type of awkward silence that would prompt someone to say, *well, it was nice meeting you,* and be on their merry way. Cas hadn't quite figured out how to talk to girls. Most of his friends had already done it. They'd already lost their virginity. He, on the other hand, was still a virgin. He wondered if girls could smell that on him. *Does Jazzie know I'm still a virgin? Just by talking to me?* Maybe that's why she'd sniffed him. Weird.

"The boys at St. Thomas are pretty cute," she said, winking at him, unexpectedly.

Cas felt heat suffuse his face and knew he'd flushed beet red.

She is so incredibly beautiful. How...why is she still talking to—

"Get off of him!" a girl yelled from the living room.

"Ah-hhhhhh!!" another girl screamed wildly.

A loud crash and harsh shouting erupted from another part of the house. Everyone who'd been knocking about in the kitchen rushed to find out what the commotion was. Cas stood watching, incredulously, at the fight between an older boy he didn't recognize and Brian Flanagan, a hothead from St. Thomas. They were grappling in the living room. Brian, an experienced wrestler, had locked the boy's neck in a crank, his grip tightening. The other boy squirmed out, escaping from the predatory hold, and shoved Brian into a few bystanders.

"Get him, Brian! Don't let him off easy!" someone shouted.

"Beat his ass, Mark!"

Mark landed a right hook directly on Brian's jaw, sending him reeling backwards. They were inches from a sideboard holding more of the family's heirlooms. Andrew hadn't had time to put away all the plates and antique vases and scurried toward the sideboard, flailing his arms in an attempt to stop the potential damage. As Andrew moved, someone sucker punched him from the left and he tumbled into the crowd. Another bystander was knocked off balance and tumbled directly into the sideboard.

Shit! Not good!

Cas wished he'd helped his friend secure the expensive fixtures before the party. Mr. Byrne was a hard-ass, and Cas wanted to keep Andrew out of serious trouble. The poor kid hadn't enjoyed a moment of his own party, and now it seemed it was already over.

Stan and Mike and a few other of his friends went to Andrew's rescue. Stan announced in the most authoritative voice he could muster the party had come to an end.

"EVERYONE, OUT! PARTY'S OVER!" Stan shouted. "Get the fuck out!"

"Out, out, out!" Mike added, his voice rising with every word.

Cas ran over to assess Andrew's injury and noticed the side of his friend's forehead had a nasty-looking, swollen lump.

There was a general feeling the party had run its course, so the guests gathered their belongings to make their way out. Cas looked around for Jazzie and Seth. He backtracked through the kitchen, but didn't see them anywhere. The house had emptied out quickly, looking like the aftermath of a Category 5 hurricane.

"Hey, did you see where the redheaded girl went?" Cas asked a girl he'd seen in the kitchen just moments before the fight. "The girl hanging out in the kitchen just a little while ago?" She shot him a perplexed look, grabbed her bag and hailed her friends who were racing out the front door.

"Wait for me!" the girl called after her friends.

As she was leaving, she turned to Cas. "I didn't see anyone here tonight with red hair, sweetheart. Bye, bye!"

Cas watched as people exited the house, the few stragglers finally making for the door, either too drunk or too stoned to manage the first rush. He should've asked Jazzie for her phone number or at least her screen name.

Damnit. He'd never see her again.

CHAPTER 3

PARLI ITALIANO?

CASIMIR WALKED through the sterile hallway of St. Thomas Preparatory, all gray paint and grayer tile. He'd just left AP history class and had less than four minutes to get to English class. Apart from when students transitioned between classes, the hallways were quiet, and you could almost hear the thrum of the fluorescent lights under the clicking and clacking of the boys' and girls' dress shoes. The cleanliness of the school was comparable to that of a hospital or a quaint church, thanks in part to the strict discipline employed there. The school's culture was militaristic. Clean. Precise. High, academic standards were almost an afterthought.

He felt a wave of anxiety, the weight of the school's expectations pressing down on him like a heavy Catholic Bible as he hurried along the corridor. Walking past a classroom, he caught an echo of Brother John's voice as he delivered a lecture to his religion class, edifying the beatitudes of a passage from the New Testament. The Brother wore his uniform: a brown soutane, a knotted waist cord, an old wooden cross hung from his neck. All the Brothers wore that uniform, and all of them seemed to look down on others who didn't wear such attire. A censorious bunch, Cas thought.

Students wore required uniform dress code. Cas made sure his tie knot was tight and tucked all the way up, flush with his collar. One company held a monopoly on the ugliest school wear for Catholic students. The boys could wear white or baby blue button-down shirts and either khaki, navy blue, or gray slacks. The material had an unfortunate rough cotton quality. If one opted for a pair of woolen slacks worn during a hot summer day, you'd better mentally prepare yourself to sweat your balls off. Cas had one pair of woolen slacks he'd worn twice in three years.

The girls could order similar shirts and they had the choice of wearing either slacks or skirts. Skirts, of course, had to be worn no more than two inches above the knee. If a girl didn't look like a nun-in-training, she wasn't wearing her skirt appropriately, as instructed. Some of the more rebellious girls would roll up their skirts at the waist and attempt to wear them above their knees, exposing a few inches of their thighs, though those courageous enough to try and challenge the school were few and far between. Defiant girls who tried were flagged, pulled out of line and instructed to lower their skirts to a more pious length. There were two female students (Cas had forgotten their names) who, despite constant warnings, would not comply. He remembered they had exceptional figures and never made it past freshman year.

Cas had heard that as recently as the 1980s, boys and girls would be paddled for committing such infractions. Up until about the late 1980s, serious corporal punishment was still in vogue at St. Thomas Preparatory and other Catholic schools around the city. *Thank Christ it isn't the eighties,*

Cas thought. *Now, we just get threatened with detentions or expulsion. Vestiges from the inquisition.*

Later that day, Cas stood in line at the school bookstore to buy the next novel he needed for his eleventh-grade English class, *Moby Dick.* He didn't know much about the novel, but his English teacher told the class they would skip around to different chapters, since there were only a few weeks left in the school year and they were on a tight schedule.

Andrew, ahead in line, purchased his copy of the novel from Brother Michael, a stocky man in his early sixties who ran the bookstore before school day commenced. Cas saw the book for the first time. It appeared to be as thick as a bible. Word around school was that the Marist Brother was an ex-Marine who'd served a few tours in the Vietnam War. *Interesting that a man with such deep faith might have also killed a lot of people in Vietnam,* Cas thought.

Looking curiously at the cover of his newly purchased copy of *Moby Dick* as he hurried to catch up to Andrew, Cas turned a few pages, flipping to the copyright page. 1851. *Why the hell do we have to read a book from 1851? Everything at this school is so goddamn old and antiquated.* He felt a surge of resentment at the school's insistence on archaic texts suffocating his desire to learn something more modern and relevant.

"Do you remember seeing that girl with the red hair at your house on Saturday?" Cas asked Andrew, in a low, suppressed whisper, moving to stand next to him. "She had red and gray hair? You couldn't've missed her."

"Gray hair? I don't think I saw her," Andrew said, glancing over at him with a frown. "White girl? What'd she look like?" He kept his voice low so they wouldn't get in trouble.

"Yeah. She was around five-five, five-six. Pretty thin. She looked like she could be on the cover of *Seventeen magazine*." Cas stared at Andrew. "How the fuck did you miss her? She was the hottest girl there."

"I don't know. You sure you weren't imagining her?" Andrew snickered. "I definitely would have remembered seeing someone who fits that description. Anyway, I was too busy trying to tame the animals who'd taken over my house... and too busy getting knocked out." Andrew sighed. "I'm sure someone saw her and can tell you what school she goes to."

"Your bump is barely noticeable now," Cas laughed, edging his index finger towards Andrew's forehead where a purplish lump, half an inch high, protruded. It looked like he had a golf ball trying to pop out of his forehead.

Andrew slapped Cas' hand away.

Cas shrugged. "It's a good thing your parents stayed in PA an extra night so we could clean the damn place up. Anyway, I asked her what school she went to. Hasn't enrolled in one yet—just moved here from New Orleans."

"New Orleans, huh?" Andrew tilted his head, looking quizzical. "That's kind of random. Not sure I've ever met anyone from there. Does she have a Southern accent?"

Cas thought for a moment. "Not really. Maybe a little—"

"Gentleman, let's move along, please." Brother Michael waved his hand, prodding the boys along from the bookstore like herd. "Be on your way to homeroom."

Cas and Andrew started towards homeroom. In a low whisper, Cas, walking with his head down, said, "She might be a part of some religious order. Possibly a cult. She said she couldn't enroll in a Catholic school but didn't explain why."

Andrew leaned in close to Cas. "You sure it's a good idea to pursue a girl like that?"

The next morning, Casimir sat in Italian class in his assigned seat, which was determined alphabetically by students' last names.

Signora Rossi stood behind her podium—a thick-boned woman in her early forties. Her brown, caring eyes sparkled behind her cat's-eye glasses. Many of her students adored her, especially the girls in the class. A stern but fair teacher, her pass rate for the state examination for all levels of Italian was ninety-eight-point-six percent—the highest pass rate for any state examination at the school. Her classroom emanated a positive energy not felt in many of the other classes. Cas enjoyed being in her class, since time seemed to slip away like the grains of sand. The students worked on one activity or another, always engaged, whether they were conjugating verbs or working on a pronunciation drill.

"Mi piace il gelato (I like ice cream)," a student in the front of the room said enthusiastically.

"Mi piace il gelato," another student repeated.

Signora Rossi's drills involved a lot of repetition, practicing conjugating verbs with common words. One student would say a phrase or a sentence out loud and the student seated behind would repeat that same phrase. The activity required students to repeat the conjugated phrase down the row of students, then continue on to the next row. It was a simple exercise, yet proved effective for learning a new language and nailing down the correct pronunciation. Signora Rossi would instruct students to switch to the *you, they, or them* form, then she would instruct the next student to switch the tense or the verb used. Students had to pay attention and be alert to avoid looking foolish in front of the entire class.

"Mi piace il diavolo (I like the devil)," Rick De Luca said, belting out the words when it was his turn.

The room fell silent. Mrs. Rossi's lesson lurched to a stop in a bad way, like a crash test dummy slamming against a wall at one hundred miles per hour. Cas looked over at Samantha, the girl who sat next to him, reading her lips as she mouthed: *What in the actual fuck?*

It was one thing to crack a tasteless joke with a substitute or a newbie teacher. It was academic suicide to crack a joke in Signora Rossi's Italian class.

It was agreed Rick De Luca was psychotic. He arrived late to first-period class every day. Any student who arrived late to St. Thomas Prep, albeit by two seconds, had to serve a JUG, short for "Justice Under God." JUGs were detentions after school, but more taxing than simply sitting in a classroom and having to stare at a book or the ceiling for an hour. Students had to perform some sort of physical activity. One JUG, in particular, required students to walk around the track outside the school for an entire hour, without breaks.

Things had softened throughout the years. The brothers would tell the students stories about how, back in the 1980s, JUGs required students to walk around the track with an unloaded rifle in 'left shoulder arms.' When the teacher or dean supervising the students called the command, the student had to transition the rifle to the alternate shoulder. Punishments like these made Cas question whether the clergy who ran the school were more interested in correcting rule breakers' behavior or whether they found sadistic pleasure in torturing adolescents. *Did they truly believe God was a merciful being? Why weren't they merciful?* he wondered. *Sure, there was a place for discipline but it seemed they savored and found pleasure in making young teenage boys and girls suffer under their judgmental watch. What else did they enjoy?* Cas wondered.

Rick was nuts. In the school year book, under class predictions, they should reserve *most likely to become a serial killer* for him. Cas recalled, in ninth grade, Rick tossed a preserved fetal pig out of the biology lab window. Mr. Keller was furious. When they'd asked him why, his response was he wanted to see if pigs could fly. Nothing happened to him afterwards. He may have served an hour detention, at most, for having committed that transgression.

Cas had been losing his faith during his tenure at St. Thomas, considering all the contradictions he'd observed. Not just the contradictions tied to his faith. Take Rick, for example. If it had been anyone else who acted the way Rick did, they'd be expelled after the first infraction or first few mishaps. He'd seen it happen to a few unfortunate freshmen. Rick's father was a wealthy New York City real estate developer who had donated tens of thousands of dollars to the school. At that point in time, it was more likely hundreds of thousands of dollars in donations, considering the number of rules his son broke on a daily basis. Hush money and bribes kept Rick enrolled at Saint Thomas Prep and everyone knew it.

———

A few months into the school year, on a dreary winter morning, Principal Richard had called Rick's father to inform him that it had been decided—his son was being expelled.

"The fuck you mean, he's expelled?" Mr. De Luca yelled, over the phone.

"We can't continue this every day, Mr. De Luca. He won't comply. And the latenesses have gotten out of hand," Richard said. "He's showing up at ten-thirty, eleven o'clock —just in time for lunch. You know how seriously we regard tardiness."

Rick Senior held an impromptu meeting with Principal Richard later that day.

He'd stormed past the secretary and barged into Richard's office like a bull in Pamplona. An English teacher, discussing a potential curriculum change, sat across from the principal when Rick Senior burst in not deferential to the office's holy facade.

"Get the fuck out of here before I throw you out the fuckin' door!" De Luca yelled.

The befuddled teacher gathered his belongings and scurried from the office with a perplexed look.

De Luca sauntered over to the door and closed it. He secured the latch, locking himself and Richard inside the sacristy-like office. He walked slowly toward Richard's desk, and glared over him for a moment before blurting, "You're going to let my kid back in school."

"Unfortunately, Mr. De Luca, your son has crossed the Rubicon."

"Here's what's gonna happen, Richard. You're going to let my son back into this fine institution." He took out a brick-shaped plastic bag and slammed it on the desk. The principal recoiled in his chair. De Luca untied the bag, unveiling bundles of hundreds of dollars, then fanned the bills in the principal's face.

The principal stared, unblinking, at De Luca and the cash. "There is nothing I can do at this point." He shook his head. "Your son has committed far too many infractions. They are now happening on a daily basis, multiple times throughout the day. As you're well aware, Mr. De Luca, we enforce strict discipline at our institution. My staff—the teachers, administration—they've all had it with him. He's failing multiple classes. There is nothing else to speak about." His voice sounded steady, though he felt as if his body was being jolted by lightning in a storm. "Now please, Mr. De Luca," he continued, "if you'd kindly leave my office. I have important matters to attend—"

De Luca edged closer toward the principal, breathing real hard.

"Excuse me. I asked you to leave," Richard said.

De Luca drew a nine-millimeter GLOCK from the inside of his jacket and aimed it at the principal's head. Richard's face turned white.

"Here's what's gonna happen. You're gonna take this bag from me and say, 'Thank you, Mr. De Luca, for your generous donation. This was all just a big misunderstanding.' Then, I'm gonna leave this office, never hear from you again about my son's *infractions*, and that'll be that." Rick Senior narrowed his eyes at him. "Understood, Principal Richard?" He pressed the gun hard against his skull, firm enough to leave an imprint.

Richard swallowed hard.

"And if anyone hears about this, you won't be receiving a 'donation' from me. Instead, you'll be receiving a slug in your cerebral cortex. You understand me?"

"Yes, yes. Okay! Your son has my blessing!" Richard cried in a tight, shaky voice.

"I want to hear you say 'your son is back in school.'"

Gasping and trembling, Richard said, "Your son...is enrolled at..." He rubbed sweat off his forehead. "St.

Thomas Preparatory. He has not been...expelled." His eyes were wide with fear. "Please remove the gun from my head. Jesus Christ."

De Luca lowered the gun and tucked it in the back of his pants, slammed his fist over the stack of cash, then stormed out.

After the incident, Principal Richard didn't want to even look at Rick again, let alone allow him to enter his office.

Just three months later, there Rick stood at the door of his office, wearing a blank look, holding a pass signed by one of his teachers.

"Signora Rossi told me to come here," Rick said, holding up the pass. He sounded as apathetic as a stroke victim.

"Wait outside; I'm dealing with something at the moment!" The principal snapped. He'd lost his last ounce of patience with Rick. At times, praising his godly soul, he would daydream he'd stab Rick in the heart and then bury his lifeless body in the school's garden. How would he do it? It wasn't possible, was it? He'd surely get caught... unless? Shrugging off these unholy thoughts, Richard rapidly gave himself the sign of the cross and repeated a silent Hail Mary.

"Did he say mi piace il diavolo?" Cas asked Samantha, after Rick was sent to the principal's office. He tried to look at her eyes. It was difficult not to take a peek at her breasts, given the way she liked to unbutton her shirt as far down as she could get by with before the teachers caught her. They seemed to always be out and his eyes just gravitated towards them.

Samantha nodded. "Do you think he's going to finally get kicked out?"

"No way. His dad will find a way to get him out of this. He always does," Cas whispered.

Casimir turned his attention back to Signora Rossi. The class transitioned seamlessly back into the lesson as if there hadn't been any disruption. Signora Rossi's years of experience had trained her to be a master at handling all types of unplanned disruptions and situations, and class resumed in quick fashion.

"Mi piace la spiaggia (I like the beach)," Signora Rossi said, her voice triumphant.

"Mi piace la spiaggia," the entire class echoed.

———

He concentrated hard on the computer screen. He'd been tracking a painting on an auction site and the bidding was coming down to the final minutes. The painting he'd been bidding on, a seventeenth century oil canvas depicting a Catholic priest preparing the Eucharist, was up to one thousand seven hundred dollars with six minutes left to go in the auction.

Richard knew Rick De Luca was probably waiting for the verdict; wondering what his punishment would ultimately be.

After several minutes of dead silence, Rick broke in, "Are you going to call my father?"

"No, I'm not," Richard muttered.

"Why not?"

He turned toward the boy. "Because your father is a psychopath and I won't be dealing with him any longer."

Rick opened his mouth as if to say something but

remained quiet. He stared at Richard with his mouth slightly agape.

"Please don't interrupt me. I'll be with you in a moment."

One minute left in the auction.

Richard's gaze remained laser focused on the computer screen.

"Are you looking up alternate schools I might be transferred to once I'm officially expelled?" Rick asked.

"Shut up," Richard said.

Twenty seconds left in the auction. The counter flashed red digits: *Seventeen. Sixteen. Fifteen. Fourteen...*

Richard pressed several keys and clicked his mouse, securing a higher bid. He was now the highest bidder. *Ten seconds left.*

He hit more keys and then enter, upping his bid.

Two thousand six hundred and ninety-nine dollars.

You were outbid flashed on the screen.

Clicking more keys and pressing enter, once more, he maxed out his bid.

Three, two, one.

You've won this auction appeared on the screen.

"Good," he whispered.

Glancing toward Rick, he found the boy staring curiously back at him. "Rick, I'd like you to return to class. Italian class should be over now," Richard said. "What class do you have now?"

"Uh, math."

"You may go now. I'm sure Sister Margaret is missing you dearly."

Rick stood up to leave and made for the door. When he got to the door jamb, he turned and said, "So, am I expelled or—"

"Get out!"

As soon as Rick left, Richard circled around his desk and locked the door. Returning to his desk, he plopped down and sank down in his leather chair. The weight of the school day wore heavily on him.

He groaned.

He opened the bottom drawer of his desk and grabbed a paper bag. Peering into the bag, he saw several bundles of hundred-dollar bills, all strapped neatly and compactly. He pulled out a bundle. He reclined in his executive chair and flipped through a stack of crisp C-notes as if thumbing through a flipbook.

Richard placed the bag of money back in his desk, then returned his attention to his computer. He opened the Tor Browser application and logged onto the *hidden wiki* website—a website on the Dark Web. In the search bar, he typed: *hitman*.

Richard stared at the webpage for a while, lost in a fog of thoughts he knew were sinful, until he finally came to and clicked out of it.

CHAPTER 4
SIBLINGS

SERVERS CLAD in long black uniforms and white aprons glided through the parlor, topping off guests' glasses with whiskey and other high-end cocktails. Other wait staff, a mix of men and women, circulated the room offering beignets, cakes, pralines, éclairs, and fruit tarts stacked high on large platters. Guests wore an array of formal gowns and suits, dancing and stirring, striving to impress one another. The Duprés were hosting Shrove Tuesday—Mardi Gras—and their mansion overflowed with the crème de la crème of New Orleans society.

Anne Dupré wore a resplendent mauve-colored silk Victorian gown, imported from England just for this event. She moved through her guests, elegantly and effortlessly, moving like women of the distinguished class have always done. Charles had paid a king's ransom for the dress but, for the Duprés, money was the least of their concerns. Charles' family had amassed a considerable fortune in real estate during the early part of the nineteenth century, leaving him an inheritance beyond imagination.

"More, monsieur?" A tall, lithe server, not more than nineteen, stood at Charles Dupré's elbow.

"You may, darlin'," he replied, winking at the cocktail waitress.

Anne Dupré frowned at her husband, before looking around the room.

A plump, middle-aged woman dressed in a pink brocade gown knocked back her cocktail. "Mmm, I ain't never tasted a Sazerac as good as this one," she said, savoring the sweet gulp.

Anne's gaze was caught by the pianist. His eyes were dark and icy and hypnotic. The man's fingers danced across the grand piano's keys with deft precision, quiet but lively music serenading her guests without being obtrusive. He'd been hired to entertain on that Shrove Tuesday evening in 1868, along with a violinist, a clarinetist, a cellist, and a harpist. The ensemble played a selection of well-known sonatas, ranging from Beethoven and Mozart to Vivaldi.

Many of the guests shifted their attention towards the pianist as the third movement of Beethoven's Moonlight Sonata was heard circling throughout the mansion's parlor.

"He's somethin' else, ain't he!" the woman in the pink gown praised, giving Anne a sideways glance. Beatrice Dubuclet was known for poaching the best cooks, servers and musicians in New Orleans party scene to make her parties the best in town. "Is he famous? How'd you find him, if you don't mind my askin'?"

"Well, now. I met..." Anne stopped and backtracked. "I saw him play when Charles and I went to Massachusetts on business a few years back. Just so happens he's relocated down south. We just hope he don't get too famous so he keeps entertainin' for us." She laughed, but her lips felt too tight to move. Shivering, she thought back to the pleasurable sensation of when Şerban sucked her blood. God, I hope he does it tonight, she thought. *It's been years since I've felt such ecstasy.*

"Does he reside in the Quarter?" Mrs. Dubuclet asked, circling the rim of her glass with one finger, her expression curious.

"He resides—" Anne caught sight of her children entering the parlor. "Colette! Jermain!" Anne took a swig from her tumbler. She wished to avoid any further discussion of her ties with Şerban. She'd already divulged too much. Her children would provide a convenient distraction. "Colette, Jermain, do come over and greet an old friend of mine."

———

Colette Dupré wobbled awkwardly towards her mother in her high heeled boots. She'd never gotten the hang of those dreaded heels, which she'd only ever use on occasions like tonight. Her ruffled dress sported a small bustle and a felt bonnet rested on top of her red curls, which were artfully arranged over one shoulder. Over her arms rested a wool shawl. She looked miserable. Hot, itchy and miserable.

Jermain Dupré stood next to his sister. They went almost everywhere together, rarely seen apart. He wore a formal suit, tailored to fit elegantly on his manly frame. He measured six foot one and, though he was only seventeen, he carried himself like a mature gentleman. It was difficult for anyone to guess what Jermain was feeling at any given moment, his face typically deadpan. Even his sister wasn't sure whether he was ever happy, sad, angry, bored, indifferent. He never showed emotion. She found his dry humor quite amusing, even though he'd claim he wasn't attempting to be humorous when she laughed.

"Do look at this marvelous gown! I simply cannot!" Mrs. Dubuclet exclaimed, reaching out to touch the fabric of Colette's dress.

"Children, this is Mrs. Dubuclet," Anne said, her tone relieved. "She and her husband are proprietors of some of the largest plantations in Louisiana."

Colette pinched at her back, trying to scratch an itchy spot she couldn't reach. "I believe I recall meeting you, Mrs. Dubuclet, when I was quite young. In any case, it is a pleasure." Colette extended her hand and shook Mrs. Dubclet's.

She then turned to her mother. "Mother, can Jermain and I retire? I wish to remove this constricting gown." She scratched through the bustle, struggling to get through to scratch her hip. "It's both tight and irritating. We desire to go upstairs and play a game of dominoes."

"You may certainly not," Anne said, her expression stern. She lowered her voice, "Have I not instilled proper manners in you? Be certain to address all of our guests and make them feel welcome. If you do not recognize one of our guests, introduce yourself and express your gratitude for their presence. Endeavor to be sociable for once."

Anne turned towards Jermain, her eyes pleading. "Do you understand, Jermain? Please encourage your sister to behave appropriately this evening."

"Yes, mother," Jermain said lightly, seeming uninterested in the conversation.

Anne looked back at Colette, her voice a mere whisper, "Engage in conversation with some of the young gentlemen present. You're not becoming any younger."

Colette remained silent, quashing the surge of anger her

mother's words provoked. She lifted her chin, not looking in her mother's direction. She wouldn't give her mother the satisfaction of seeing her upset. Instead, she hoped Mother would get tired of speaking nonsense to her and get dragged away—become distracted—by one of their other guests.

Colette knew Jermain didn't fight their mother when she asked him to do something. Since Colette often found it difficult to please her, Jermain had admitted to her it would make both their lives easier if he just adapted to the circumstances. Everyone who lived in the mansion—Colette, Jermain, the house staff—knew their parents' relationship was on edge and they slept in separate rooms. Within the past few months, Ma and Pa barely spoke to each other and, if they did, it was regarding important matters about her and her brother, such as matters concerning their education. Or Colette's potential suitors. They didn't seem to worry too much about Jermain's prospects. It was Jermain who helped ease the tension—ease his mother's stress. He'd told Colette on many occasions that it simply made life more bearable around the house.

Outsiders who peered in should have seen nothing but joy, peace, and love. Inside the mansion's walls was something quite different. Perhaps something more closely resembling a murky swamp of deceit, scandal, and lies. Colette wondered if a single spark of love still flickered between them two.

Mrs. Dubuclet's eyes flickered to Colette's necklace, a delicate gold chain adorned with an 18-karat gold locket, featuring a European-cut diamond and opals. It hung around her neck, seeming to radiate a golden manna.

Mrs. Dubuclet's gaze was transfixed upon the piece. "What a marvelous necklace, Colette!" she said, her fingers instinctively reaching out, nearly making contact.

Colette recoiled before Mrs. Dubuclet's fingers arrived.

Creepy old matron, Colette thought. She put her hand over her necklace, protectively, her cheeks flushed red.

Mrs. Dubuclet smiled, her hand returning to her side awkwardly.

Anne cut in and said, "It was a gift from her uncle. He travels from France and always brings her delightful keepsakes whenever he visits."

Colette looked at her mother with wide eyes.

"This was from Uncle Lucien? I thought—"

Anne cut her off. "Yes, sweetheart. It was."

Mrs. Dubuclet changed the subject. "How lovely! Which of your children possesses the musical ear?"

"They are both quite musically inclined," Anne said.

Colette frowned at her enthusiasm.

"How delightful," the other woman said. "Why not take a turn at the piano?"

"That sounds like a great idea. I'll speak to the pianist and see if it would be agreeable."

They turned to look at Şerban, the pianist. He had taken a break and stood on the side of the Grand Piano smoking a corncob pipe. A violinist was performing a solo piece, allowing the other players to break for a few minutes.

———

Anne glided through the parlor, past her German porcelain. Her steps were small, her head held high, her shoulders arched. Her bustle bounced behind her with each step. Her face, along with the soft paraffin lamps that burned, illuminated the parlor. The candlelight's softness made all their guests glow a supernatural chestnut red that gave everything a dreamlike quality. She took her time, hoping everyone would turn and look and marvel at her dress. Why else throw a party if one couldn't wear a splendid dress?

"Excuse me..." Anne said, as she approached Şerban.

"Yes? What do you need?" Şerban's accent was thick, his manner indifferent. She presumed he was Italian, but the man could have easily hailed from the Austro-Hungarian Empire or some other part of the world, if she were to guess. He wore a jet-black suit, the same color as his long hair and unruly goatee.

"Might I ask you for a favor, Şerban?"

Şerban stared at her with disdain.

"If you must insist on inflicting this further aggravation upon me, then, by all means, disgorge your request," Şerban said tightly, his tone as sharp as a blade.

Anne floundered at his brusqueness. She thought he looked forward to being there—to playing at their home. That was the reason she'd invited him in the first place. It was clear he did not reciprocate her feelings. The manner in which he'd addressed her was rather unpleasant. She felt hot and sweaty underneath her makeup.

"Would it be agreeable if my children took a turn at the piano? They've some practice and the guests would like to hear them play."

He inclined his head in agreement, but his expression of disdain didn't change.

I've made a mistake, haven't I? she thought, a shiver running down her spine.

"I wish to speak with you privately, Madam Dupré."

She looked around, her hands clenching. "Privately?"

"Yes," he said, glancing down at her breasts. "Is there a suitable location for a private conversation?"

"Now? I intend to watch my children perform."

"It shall be either now or never," he said.

Despite her unease, she could deny him nothing. Did he want her? She wanted him, but his expression told her nothing. She hoped he would suck her blood again. It had been several years since he'd done that, and she missed the sensation. Her body trembled as she raised a shaky hand to the thready pulse at her throat. "Meet me upstairs in fifteen minutes. Third door down the corridor on the left. I shall wait for you there." She lifted her chin and met his eyes for one brief moment. "After I listen to my children play a movement or two." Anne turned and departed.

———

Şerban drew the crowd's attention. "Ladies and gentlemen," he said. "We have two very special guests who will be performing for you tonight. Sir Jermain and Madam Colette, would you please come up to the piano?" He beckoned the children over towards the piano.

"Oh, God," Colette said.

She turned to her brother. "I don't feel like playing in front of these old crows," she said. She was a few weeks out of practice and, now, she had been summoned to play in front of New Orleans aristocracy. She touched her necklace and looked around the room as Jermain led her to the piano. There were a few younger gentlemen in the crowd. Potential suitors. How embarrassing. Perhaps she could still escape without anyone noticing.

Jermain sat down at the piano and pulled her down next to him.

"I hate you," she muttered, stretching her fingers and cracking her knuckles. "What shall we play?"

Jermain grinned. "I believe this evening calls for Chopin's Waltz...in E minor."

"You would like to see Mother and Father's guests prance, wouldn't you?" She laughed, leaning close to his ear so no one else could hear.

"It wouldn't hurt to liven up the old bunch, would it? It would serve as a wellness check to ensure their hearts are beating and they are still among the living," Jermain said. "If they begin to gavotte, we will know they're still living and breathing. If they remain as motionless as your porcelain doll collection, we shall summon the coroner to assess their vital signs, or perhaps arrange for their transfer to St. Louis Cemetery." The young man maintained a deadpan expression. Always deadpan.

———

Şerban seemed to have cast a soporific spell on the unsuspecting crowd, disappearing from the parlor room in shape-shifting flashes, like a wraith. The guests would not remember he had ever been there on that consequential evening. Fifteen minutes later, a powerful medieval spell would produce yawns in the parlor and all the guests would begin to say their goodbyes.

———

Charles Dupré stood near the Dubuclets and raised his drink towards his children.

"Gather 'round and lend your ears. You're 'bout to hear the sweetest music this side of the Mississippi, played by none other than my own flesh and blood. Watch close, for these young'uns will surely charm your very souls."

After the children played the waltz, they transitioned to Beethoven's Symphony No. 7, II. Allegretto in A minor.

The guests quieted their loud chatter to a low murmur. A few of the guests admitted, through whispers, they had not heard such a lovely rendition of the piece played on a piano until then. Colette and Jermain's fingers danced along the keys and played chords without a single error; the vibrations flowed through the guests, mesmerizing each listener, one by one, in sublime reverie. Then, in a few minutes, the guests began to yawn.

———

Upstairs, Şerban walked down the dark corridor and entered the third door on the left. Once inside, he flipped the latch to prevent anyone else from entering.

Inside the maid's room, Anne sat on the bed and cried into her handkerchief. Two flickering candles cast long, dancing shadows across her tear-stained face. She had slipped into one of her manic episodes. They were happening more and more frequently, sometimes lasting for several hours, other times days, especially if she'd run out of her opium pills. Anne had been one week without her opium and her mental state was oscillating like a seesaw.

"Do you know what today is, Madam?"

"What is today, Şerban?" Mrs. Dupré asked, tears pouring down her rosy cheeks.

"Today is Shrove Tuesday. A Day for feasting and getting fat." A sly smile shifted across his face, contorting it in an ugly way.

"Did you try the beignets?" She was too busy crying and didn't look in his direction, embarrassed to be sobbing so much in his presence.

"It is also a day to confess one's sins. Will you be

confessing your sins, Mrs. Dupré?" He laughed, his words mocking.

She sniffled, raising her chin a bit. "I have nothing to confess. I'm a godly woman."

"Godly woman," he repeated with a cruel sneer. "I find you to be quite amusing. I can read your mind. You are wanting to kill yourself, and that is a mortal sin."

"Was I wrong in hirin' you tonight?" Anne raised her tearstained face, searching his expression. "Did I think you wanted to see me?"

"Right and wrong...that's a matter of perspective."

Anne frowned, looking befuddled. "Why all the riddles? I thought you came down here to be near me. To be with me. I invited—"

Şerban approached her.

"What do you want from me?" She shrunk back on the bed, drying her eyes with the back of her hands, her handkerchief soaked.

"Lovely, Anne...What I want from you is..." His nostrils flared. "To answer something for me."

———

Anne cowered as Şerban grew nearer. She could go no further, trapped on the edge of the bed. Why did he look so much older all of a sudden? His visage had altered. His face appeared, to Anne, like a canvas hacked with the history of a man who'd engaged in years of slaughter and warfare. A monstrous, evil hunger blazed in his eyes, Anne thought, a hunger that could only be satiated by spilling blood and reveling in suffering.

Anne averted her eyes, unable to bear the sight, her mind entering mania.

"I will give you a choice... and you will have only one chance to decide." In the deepening twilight of the bedroom, his face contorted into a mask of horror, his voice dropping even lower. "There is only life, death, and something in between, which I have been blessed with. A gift. Eternal life. You may choose between the eternal or—"

Anne tilted her head up. She didn't want to look, but she had to. Her face turned pale white—as white as a sheet—at the sight of his monstrous face. A gasp escaped her.

"Why? Oh, why?" Anne screamed.

He covered her mouth with long, cadaverous fingers, cold against her heated skin.

"Death." His eyes blazed red as he said the word. "Which would you like?" The words carried a wickedness that compressed her bones. "If you choose eternal life, your children will die. If you choose death, they will be saved."

"Why my family?"

Desperation clawed at her stomach at the thought of any danger to her children. She would not let this man, this thing hurt them. Not ever.

He leaned over her, his face menacing. "Your children—their blood—they are the progeny I require. Your daughter—"

"Colette," Anne said, in a very low, choked voice. Her eyes wide with fear.

"Yes, Colette." Her daughter's name sounded naughty on his lips. "The lovely princess is able to wear the necklace, but you are not. The necklace was originally for you, was it not?"

Anne tried to pull away from Şerban but he drew her closer.

She shook uncontrollably. "Yes," she said. "How did you

know? Please, leave her out of this. Don't harm my children," she pleaded, forcing to get the words out.

"You are weak. Your mind is soft, damaged." His dead, red eyes stared down at her. "You're not fit for my blood."

Şerban drew Anne's neck towards his mouth. The sight of Şerban's fangs froze her veins—paralyzed her body. She wasn't able to fight him off. She couldn't.

His fangs dug brutally into the side of her neck. Pain blasted through her body. The vibrations of the piano were but a murmur emanating from below. The ecstatic and mesmerized guests were oblivious to the demon in their presence just one floor above their drunken heads.

In her stupor, she saw the details of a crest she'd seen before on Şerban when they first met. It was a coat of arms —the left side a crescent moon above a six-pointed star; the right side six horizontal stripes. The crest was black, faded, and barely visible, almost camouflaged into his coat.

"Oh, Lord, spare my children," Anne said, too exhausted to resist, succumbing to God's horrendous will.

The pain roiled through Anne's flesh; sharp pangs of agony jolted her tissue, like a snake's bite ravaging her flesh. A sharp, electric pain engulfed her nerves, she reeled between an awakened agony and a hazy state of half-conscious drowse.

The vampire's face had grown older. He, or more accurately, it (was it even living?), had morphed into a relic not one bit resembling the pianist who'd entered the Dupré home earlier that evening. His eyes were sunken into his skull; a sequence of cracks and creases furrowed his forehead, cheeks, and chin. He appeared older than any human, and his breath reeked of human rot. An artifact from a museum, somehow reanimated.

The vampire thrust inside her and she felt herself

growing lifeless, her soul fleeing her corpse-like frame. He drained all the blood from her body and continued his assault. Just before her last breath escaped from her stiff, blue lips, Anne stared at the veins on the vampire's face as they pulsated out and in, out and in, like worms burrowing inside his gray head. The newly ingested blood coursed, maelstrom-like, through Şerban's vessels, and a glow began to edge her vision. Anne's eyes closed peacefully, her limbs and appendages going still, as her mind drifted into the cold, empty abyss.

———

Much later that evening, Mary, a young housekeeper who lived with the Dupré family, stumbled into the servant's bedroom and found Anne's lifeless body strewn across the bed. Sprayed blood discolored the white bed sheets, pillows, and nearby walls. The mangled corpse and the spilled blood caused her to let out a shrill scream and then faint.

Charles Dupré, who'd fallen asleep on a chair in the parlor, awoke, startled by the maid's scream. He spilled the half-filled whiskey glass he'd been holding all over himself. A heaviness formed in his stomach. The scream sent a bitter chill through his body, turning on a primal alarm inside him, prompting him to retrieve his rifle from the gun safe. He had stored it packed with powder—heavily loaded in case their family was ever in danger. Though he didn't partici-pate in the War Between the States, he was an experienced hunter and marksman, often going out to hunt wild game with his close confidants.

He hurried up the stairs and stumbled into the maid's room, seeing the terrified housekeeper laying on the floor next to the bed. Charles' heart hammered as he took in the hideous site, stomach wrenching as the air in his chest vanished.

"Anne!" He dropped the rifle to race over to where she lay and touched her forehead. There was blood all over her once flawless skin and it already felt cold. "No-no-no-no-no! God, No!...Please!"

They'd experienced their troubles and hardships but, upon seeing Anne's corpse, with lacerations carved all over her body, Charles lost all hope, all peace. Her once beautiful skin and body had become immutably unrecognizable.

This isn't my wife.

The mattress and all of the bed clothing was saturated with blood. And there she lay—her deformed pale body—a dried-out cadaver, nothing more than skin, meat, and bone. Nothing to animate it, make it look more human.

Charles Dupré mustered all his strength, sucked in several deep breaths and regained his composure. He looked around the room, studying his surroundings, looking for clues to help him understand what had transpired.

Who did this? Is the assailant still in the house? This monster could still be inside the house, he thought. *My children...*

He glanced at the window. Closed. The door was the only entrance and exit. After all, they were on the second floor, and no ladder or trellis leaned outside to help someone escape.

Mary, who'd come to, bawled beside Anne's lifeless, bloodied corpse.

"Did you see anything? Did anyone leave the room?" he asked Mary, still out of breath. He found it impossible to find any air in the room. Beads of sweat lined his face.

Mary shook her head, unable to produce any words as she crouched motionless in shock, muttering.

"Mary!" Charles lifted her to her feet and shook her. "Mary, help me."

The shock of finding Anne's butchered corpse had shattered her cognitively.

Picking up his rifle, Charles signaled for the young housekeeper to follow him into the hallway. She didn't move, so he pulled her with him, guiding her out of the room.

"Stay behind me. We can't be certain of the creature's whereabouts," he said, his voice almost a whisper. "It could be anywhere in this cursed house!"

Charles hurried down the hallway towards the children's bedrooms with rifle in hand, surveying the dark hall. Colette's room was two doors down their wallpaper-lined corridor. Jermain's, the door after. They arrived at Colette's bedroom and found the door ajar. He peered inside the dark room, attempting to see whether the children were inside before entering.

"Colette, Jermain, are you in here?" he whispered. His stance was low as he entered the bedroom, as if his knees were tied by a cord. Nothing. He had to find his children and find them quickly. His movements were stealthy, but urgent as he moved down the hall to check Jermain's empty room. His heart raced just as fast. He checked Jermain's bedroom and it was empty. *Are they still alive?*

"Mr. Dupré, I've seen the children sometimes play and hide in the basement." The frightened housekeeper could barely speak.

"Follow me." He motioned her toward the staircase he'd run up earlier.

They made their way down the shadowy stairs, trying as best they could to not make the wood beneath them creak any more than it already did. Every creak meant a higher chance of death.

The house felt wrong. Something watched them in the dark, and it made the skin crawl on the back of his neck.

Where are you, children? What beast could have done that to my Anne? I need to find the children and get them out! Charles moved his head from side to side, searching every nook and cranny as they moved further into the house. His thoughts raced as he strained to open his eyes wider, hyper alert as he and Mary traversed through the main hall. Candle sconces lined the hall, the only source of light, casting pendulous shadows ahead and behind them, seeming to take on a life of their own. Tucking his gun, Charles took a brass candle from a table in the foyer and lifted it tightly in his grasp, illuminating their way.

They arrived at the basement door, the only place they hadn't yet checked. Charles always avoided the basement, with its cold, damp walls and muffled silence. The brass door knob was bloodied. Untucking his shirt, Charles used it to turn the knob and open the door. Sepulchral sounds of pain rose from the darkness, faint but frightening. Turning back to Mary, he leaned toward her and whispered, "Go. Go next door and get help."

"Yes, Mr. Dupré." Mary's lips quivered as she nodded, before running towards the front door.

Charles wiped sweat from his brow and stepped onto the first step, pausing for a moment before moving down the stairs one careful step at a time, his gun at the ready. His panic heightened with each footfall, as the chilling air rose to surround him. He prayed it weren't his children's painful cries he heard. As he moved lower into the basement, Charles felt as if he were Dante Alighieri, descending into a lower region of Hell, where the punishments became more severe, the sights more gruesome, and where hope was a chimerical notion.

By the time he found his children, Jermain slumped cross-legged towards the back of the cellar near the cast iron furnace, petting his sister's hair as she lay across his lap, trying to muffle her sobs against his jacket. His face was streaked with dirt and tears, and his hand moved automatically to comfort his sister although his eyes were vacant pools of pain. Charles set the candle down next to his children, shining life onto their pallid faces, and tucked his gun under his left arm.

His heart jumped into his throat when the pianist spoke from the shadows. "It is too late, Mr. Dupré." Charles shifted his gun back into position and turned in a circle, but Şerban was nowhere to be seen. "I've already tasted their blood and they... they've had a taste of mine." A piercing wind swept Charles as the pianist spoke, his voice ricocheting off the walls around them. "It is only a matter of time."

"WHERE ARE YOU, COWARD!" Charles shouted, hands tight on the rifle as he whirled around, searching every shadow. "Show yourself."

His demand was met with total silence.

Sucking in a deep breath, Charles turned his attention back to his children. "What has he done to you?" Shifting his gun to his left hand, he stroked Colette's hair to the side and saw two bloody punctures on her neck, still oozing.

He lifted his head to check on his son. Charles saw he, too, had similar marks on his neck, each about half a centimeter in diameter. Two almost perfect holes, the blood dripping from them making his white-collared shirt ruddy.

Charles gasped and made the sign of the cross to ward off the evil he perceived around them. Surely only the devil could do such things in a godly household, and to children, no less, after taking their mother from them in violence.

A fluttering mass dropped from the ceiling and sprang onto Charles' back. He felt a sharpness at his neck and jerked, attempting to detach the prowler from his back. Hammering the thing's head with the butt of his rifle, he threw it off him. Once free from its hold, Charles spun around and fired.

His ears rang with the thunderous sound of all the bells and knells in Louisiana.

He had packed the chamber with extra powder in the event their family were ever in danger. They were in danger now.

A boom echoed throughout the basement; a piece of the figure frayed in the dark. Charles reached into his jacket pocket to reload the rifle with another round of black powder, trying not to fumble in his actions. His hands shook, but he managed to load it in quick order, and fired again. The second shot blasted the thing's head. A piece of its cranium—shattered bone and a crimson mass—smacked against the cellar wall nearby. Charles saw, in the candle's weak glow, the thing was now missing the top right part of its skull. Somehow, still alive, it shrieked in the dark, and moved about chaotically. It collapsed, then scrambled to pick itself up again, but fell back down. The thing's movements followed no logic.

Charles toggled his weapon and attempted to load it with more gunpowder. He touched his neck and saw red on his fingertips. He'd been bitten in the struggle. He did not feel any pain but, in an instant, weariness struck him and his eyes began to close. The last thing he saw before his eyelids shut and he keeled over was his son rushing towards him.

"Father!" Jermain said, staggering towards him with his hand outstretched.

Charles' eyelids flickered, and the smell of coppery blood and damp earth filled his nostrils. The candle was nearly out, barely illuminating a small radius in the cellar. Jermain's hands were warm against his arms, and he felt his son tremble as he sobbed. Charles attempted to move, but was unable to. He let out a deep breath, using all the energy he could muster to speak.

"Your sister, how is she?"

Charles looked up, relief transparent on his face. "She feels cold as ice and she's sweatin' somethin' fierce," Jermain said. "Father, I don't know what to do."

"Is that *thing* dead?" Charles asked, managing to lift his hand for a moment to point in the general direction of the thing he'd shot.

Jermain squinted into the darkness, an involuntary shudder moving his shoulders. "I reckon so. Ain't moved since you shot it."

Charles looked around. The cellar was dark and quiet. There were no signs of the pianist; no signs of that thing. He grabbed Jermain's arms and tried to sit up, finally managing to prop himself against the wall with his son's help.

"Listen to me," he said, maintaining his grip on Jermain's left arm. "I need you to go and get help. Go look for Mary. She went to the neighbor's. Can you manage...," he said, his voice strained and low. "...to do that?"

"I'll go now," Jermain said, nodding.

Charles took the gunpowder bag from his jacket pocket and handed it to Jermain, motioning toward the rifle that lay on the floor.

"Load this now..." Agonizing pain stopped him for a moment. He took a deep breath. "Go."

———

Jermain began to load the rifle, but a stir and a ruffling sound made them both jump. He turned and held the candle up, realizing it was Colette who'd stirred in the dark. Jermain went over to her.

"Here, take this." He placed the rifle in Colette's hands, then set the candle next to her. "I'm goin' to fetch help. You might need it, you hear?"

"Okay," Colette said weakly.

Charles interrupted them. "Jermain, go. Now."

Jermain sprang up and made for the stairs. He'd climbed only a few stairs when something snatched hold of his ankle through a space between a tread. Dagger-like fingernails tore into his leg. The pain made Jermain howl. He shook his foot loose as the nails raked flesh and muscle off his lower leg. The disfigured vampire, with the top part of its head missing, advanced, trying to latch its maw onto Jermain's neck. Though the vampire had lost the top part of its head, Jermain could see, in the candle's dim light, the shadowy head had retained its mouth and sharp fangs. Jermain cursed, tripped backwards, and fell off the stairs with the beast lunging after him.

Another deafening roar exploded in the cellar, and Jermain looked toward his family. His sister Colette, pale but determined, gripped the rifle and fired a round, hitting the beast in the chest. It was dark, nearly impossible to see, but the shot had found its mark. Their father, an avid hunter, had trained his children well, taught them to track game and kill prey in the Bayou. Their training served Colette well on this grim evening.

The beastly thing floundered and made a clamorous wailing sound that tapered off until all the sound was swallowed away by the coal-like darkness of the desolate cellar as it dropped to the ground.

Wasting no time, Jermain got himself up the stairs and hobbled out of the house. Sharp daggers of pain shot through his damaged leg and the side of his neck, where he'd been savagely bitten. He reached the neighbor's front door, his blood pooling on the front porch.

Mrs. King, who'd been a guest at the Dupré party earlier that evening, opened the front door. Holding an oil lamp, her expression turned to one of abject horror as she looked at Jermain. Mary, the Dupré's housekeeper, stood behind Mrs. King and gasped in terror, her trembling hands going to her mouth.

"What in the world, boy?" Mrs. King exclaimed, disbelief coloring her tone. "What happened to you? Who did this to you?"

Jermain shook his head, trying to focus on his mission. "They don't have much time. We need the doctor."

He could barely stand. Mrs. King and Mary's eyes panned to the holes where blood dribbled from the wounds on his neck.

"They're in the basement. I won't be able to help my father up the stairs." Jermain grimaced, the pain roiling through his body. "I can manage with Colette, but I'll need some help getting him up the stairs."

Mary brought Jermain a cloth for his wound. He took it and pressed it tightly against his neck.

"Hush, hush, now. Don'tcha worry yo'self about none o' that. Once he arrives, the doctor will fix you right up," Mary said, wrapping another bandage around his leg, her fingers trembling as she tried to make it hold the edges of the wound together.

"Mary, what happened to my mother?" he asked, focusing on her face to keep from crying out in pain.

Mary didn't respond. She simply stared at Jermain with sad, watery eyes and continued to tighten the bandage.

"Mary?" he asked again.

There was a long moment of silence before she said, "Don't you worry none 'bout that, Jermain." She tied the bandage off and sat back to inspect her work. "This should do fo' the time bein'."

Mrs. King returned from inside the house. "Jermain, you stay here. We'll look after yer pa and sister."

"I'm going." Jermain pushed himself up, unsteady but determined. It was his job to save his family, not theirs. "And then I'll find my mother."

Having the other men with him bolstered his courage, but his body didn't want to obey him. By the time they reached his house, he staggered up the stairs, gasping.

Once inside, near the cellar door, Jermain noticed the faint odor of gunpowder and burnt flesh. A heavy tiredness enveloped him and finding the nearest settee, he curled up on it and fell asleep.

CHAPTER 5

FEVER

COLETTE AWOKE LATER THAT AFTERNOON. She was lying in her bed in a pool of her own sweat. Mary wiped her damp forehead with a soft cloth, singing to her softly. 'Oh! Susanna.'

The piercing sun splashed through her bedroom window. Colette turned her head away from the light and writhed under the covers.

"Mary, could you close the curtains?" Colette cried, placing her hand over her eyes. "It's too bright."

"Sure thing, honey." Mary closed the curtains, and the room, now wrapped in darkness, became more soothing, more bearable for Colette.

"It hurts when I talk," Colette said. "My throat."

"Try to rest. You've been through a lot," Mary said. "Mrs. King summoned some help to care for your brother and Pa."

"How are they? Where's my mother?"

"Jermain looks pale and sick. Same way you look. We've called the doctor. Should be arriving later this evening or tomorrow morning." Mary stroked Colette's hair gently, moving strands away from her face. "We think you all have a bad fever."

"Yellow fever?" Colette asked.

"Possibly, dear. You just rest now." Mary stroked Colette's forehead with the back of her hand. "You're mighty cold. Some rest should fix you right up," Mary said, smiling down at her.

Colette had a terrible nightmare that afternoon. She was back in the cellar, the rifle aimed at the pianist. She pressed her finger down on the trigger and the bullet shot out of the barrel. She followed it in slow motion. Time had slowed down. The bullet spun fiercely and appeared to expand as it surged through the air. Just before the bullet made contact with the pianist's torso, he vanished. Colette felt long, icy fingers wrap around her face. The fingers turned to powerful cords, almost vein-like. The pressure increased until she could no longer bear it, forcing her to drop the rifle. Her head was tilted sideways and in another fleeting moment, she felt an explosion of pain on the side of her neck. She tried to fight whoever, or whatever, had attacked her from behind. She felt her veins being depleted of blood, becoming shriveled cords that were useless to her body. In another deep breath, a warm sensation filled her from within. Her veins were pumped with fresh blood. She could see the red-hot liquid pumping through, filling out the various layers of tissue, warming her up as if liquid iron were coursing through her.

"Colette." She heard a voice call out from very far away. "Colette." It was a tin echo—a familiar voice she recognized. She opened her eyes. The voice, now much closer and soothing, was Jermain's. He stood over her at the foot of the bed. His skin was very pale, much whiter than she'd remembered it ever being. She rubbed her eyes and wondered if she saw, for a moment, his blue veins showing through his translucent skin. She glimpsed the bandage that had been wrapped around the side of his neck.

"Are we dead?" she asked.

"No, we're not. How are you feeling?"

"It's difficult to describe. I'm feeling very tired. I just want to sleep. It's a grueling effort just to talk." She sighed. "It's difficult to keep my eyes open. How are you?"

"Same as you."

It seemed there was something Jermain wanted to say, but he hesitated.

"Jermain, what is it?"

"Mother," he said, then let out a choke.

"What happened?" Colette sat up in bed. "What's happened to Mother?"

"We've lost her, Cole. She was murdered," he said, sobbing, then placed his cold, shaky hand on Colette's forearm. "Butchered," he added. "That awful beast."

Colette's body crumpled in the bed and she clutched her face with both hands and cried. "Oh, God. Oh, my God. Please, no!"

Jermain's face began to blur as tears filled her eyes.

———

Jermain stared on apprehensively as the doctor pried Charles' eyelids open, examining each eye carefully. Charles' eyes were rheumy. His father, Jermain thought, looked decayed and infinitely old. The doctor had been quiet, which told Jermain there was nothing he would really be able to do for his father.

"Mr. Dupré," the doctor said. "Could we get you some food?"

Mary frowned. "He hasn't touched a scrap of food since... well, I ain't sure exactly when," she said.

"I ain't hungry," Charles answered, then turned his head away from them.

Jermain hadn't eaten anything for a long time either. He tried to remember the last time he'd eaten anything substantial, but he couldn't pinpoint when exactly that had been.

After a few days, he and Colette expressed their hunger in secret to one another. Jermain felt as if his stomach was beginning to eat itself. One evening he attempted to eat salted beef that Mary had prepared for him, but he threw it right back up. The same thing happened to Colette. She couldn't hold down any food, either. Mary had witnessed them regurgitate their meals. Jermain thought Mary may have been contemplating leaving the house. He'd heard her praying under her breath. He figured it was just a matter of time before poor old Mary would abandon them, escape their cursed home, especially after she'd observed them feeding on rats. But she never left. He'd find her praying for them, muttering prayers of deliverance, attempting to expel the demons that had clawed their reins on the Duprés; summoning the demons to release their hold on the family's souls. Mary had brought up the idea of inviting a priest into the home to conduct an exorcism on Charles, but Jermain fought against such an idea, and made her promise to never do such a thing. He paid her handsomely for her loyalty and dedication to the family. Mary cared for and stuck by them until she passed away of old age in 1882. She never once asked Jermain nor Colette why they never aged.

. . .

Jermain was the first one to kill a human—a mortal. It happened almost accidentally. One of Father's business associates had been visiting from Vacherie. He would drop in seldomly, once or twice a year. The man was never able to hide his horror when he'd set eyes on Charles. He'd bring his assistant with him—a nineteen-year-old apprentice. Jermain would enclose himself with his father's associates in the gallery and negotiate loans. He would sign off on the dotted line, and they'd receive money—enough to hold them over for several months, sometimes a year. He hadn't realized, however, what the ramifications would be. Charles left it up to Jermain to handle the real estate dealings, being too sickly to turn his mind to such matters and growing ever more petulant as his condition worsened.

It was a hot August evening when the associate and Jermain were finishing up their meeting in the gallery. The associate shook Jermain's hand, and said, "Well, Jermain. That about does it. We won't be coming down this way anymore." He smiled, then turned and shuffled several documents into his leather bag. To his apprentice, he said, "Let's go."

"What do you mean?" Jermain asked. "What do you mean by that? You'll be back in a few months, right?"

"What I mean, Jermain, is there's nothing else to sign over. There are no more loans to write. Your father—your family—has drunk the last drop from the well."

Jermain was at a loss for words.

"I don't understand," Jermain said. "My father has a vast portfolio of real estate holdings. He has properties all over Louisiana. Many up in New England as well. What do you mean there's nothing else to sign over?" He felt hot and sick.

"What I mean, kid, is it's over," the associate said, tipping his hat toward Jermain, then pushed past him.

Jermain stood frozen, dazed, trying to make sense of what he'd heard.

The two men left his home.

Later that evening, Jermain made his way over to the hotel where they were lodging. He figured he'd make a last-ditch effort to salvage whatever deed or stock to which his family might still be duly entitled. They couldn't have lost *everything*.

Jermain knocked on the room door. The associate opened, and when he'd realized who it was, he pushed Jermain out into the dimly lit corridor.

The older gentleman grabbed Jermain by his shirt collar and said, "Did you not understand what I said to you earlier? Don't ever bother me or come looking for me again. Our business dealings have come to an end."

Jermain could smell the alcohol on the man's breath.

"If you ever follow me again, I'll make sure to teach you a lesson you'll never forget," the man said, shoving Jermain backward.

Jermain lunged and swatted his nails across the man's throat. Blood sprayed into his face and some of it got in his mouth. The blood tasted warm, sending a satisfying buzz through Jermain's body. In seconds, Jermain bared his fangs, knocked the old man to the ground, and dug his teeth into his neck. He sucked and drained the man.

Jermain released his teeth and glanced at the apprentice, who stood watching, his back against the wall, his eyes wide with terror. He didn't want to chance there being any witnesses, so he pounced on the younger man and sucked his blood as well.

He noticed how, immediately after, his vision became clearer.

As Jermain fled from the hotel, the inky night felt more real, more visceral. Flying across rooftops, he glimpsed tiny details through the small apartment windows. He saw so clearly the soft candles on the windowsills; the meager mortals moving about, resting in their homes; and he smelled the motley crew of odors.

Jermain also noticed his increased speed, so much so, people were oblivious to him as he rushed past them on Rampart Street. That night, he gazed at the moon and it appeared that her silver face was smiling down at him, seeming as if she were winking her approval at his transformation.

On a cool January night, Jermain brought Colette to a narrow alley in the Quarter, where poor men strolled in the shadows. It was a place they would never dare find themselves in had they not been turned to vampires.

"It's time I teach you to hunt, to feed for yourself," Jermain said. "Come. Follow."

Jermain scaled rapidly up an exterior staircase, and his sister followed.

"See that man there?" Jermain pointed toward an old beggar leaning against an exposed brick wall. "That's the type we have to hunt."

He climbed down from the rooftop and, seconds later, the old man shrieked. Jermain felt the man's blood rush into his mouth. He looked up at the rooftop and saw Colette peering over the edge of the building, looking frightened. "Get down here, will you?" Jermain called out.

Colette hesitated, then she began her descent. He knew

she loathed heights. When she finally reached Jermain, he turned the beggar's neck toward her, and showed her where to dig her fangs.

"I don't want to," she protested, shaking her head.

"You must." Jermain waved his hand, telling her to hurry. "Let's go, we have to be in and out. Lingering around for too long, that's how we'll get seen."

Colette dug her fangs into the side of the man's neck and drank his blood. She felt the warm blood pump through her body. Her skin felt hot. A visceral pleasure coursed through her.

"Much better than those disgusting rats," she said, as she disengaged her fangs. Then, she sank back into his neck and drained the man nearly until his death.

The years and decades passed. The seasons slipped through the fledgling vampires' fingers. Jermain told Colette and his father they'd lost all of their family's wealth and were now left penniless. He speculated that the shock Father experienced after he'd learned they'd lost everything had fueled his decline in health. By the end of the nineteenth century, they had been removed from their mansion on Rampart Street, and were forced to relocate to a cramped and decrepit dwelling.

Jermain stood in the gloom of the studio apartment, gazing at Colette. She was tracing patterns on the grimy windowpane, a look of profound sadness on her face. Her beauty was the only thing untouched by the squalid conditions of their new dwelling. How ironic it was they now possessed supernatural powers and abilities, yet they had no money, rags for clothing, and a ticking clock in the form of their dying father. Jermain was a vampire now, but he was also a son. How could they provide for their father when they couldn't even provide for themselves? How could they care for him when their very nature now demanded they hunt for survival? Jermain felt the cold logic of their new existence pressing in, and as he watched his sister, he knew he was the one who had to find the answers. He just wasn't sure where to begin.

CHAPTER 6
THE AXEMAN

THE GRUELING AFTERNOON heat had made the fifteen-minute news conference seem like two hours, but now, Chief of Police Frank Mooney was more focused on the photographs his officer handed him as they headed back to the station.

He shook his head. "Between mothers losing their children during the war, this influenza that's just started, and now the Axeman, it's a wonder people in this city haven't lost their joy. *Laissez les bons temps rouler* (Let the good times roll)." Mooney glanced at the officer before returning his attention to the photos. "I suppose that's why most folks aren't having it with the closures."

"There's something else you should know about, Chief." The officer looked worried which, in turn, worried the chief.

He sighed. *More bad news?* "What else?"

"We've found more bodies." The officer kept his gaze on the road.

Mooney sat up straighter in his seat. "The Axeman?"

The officer shook his head, his eyes still on the road. "We don't think so."

"What do you mean?" Mooney's full attention was on the man driving.

"We think these murders and the Axeman murders are unrelated," the officer said, his voice not quite steady. "We're still uncertain whether the assailant is human or—"

Mooney felt heat flood his cheeks as he interrupted, "Or what? Human or fucking what?"

"Or animal."

Mooney glowered at the officer, his hands fisted around the photos. "What the hell do you mean, animal?"

"Well, see these wounds here." The officer took his gaze off the road for a second and pointed to one of the photographs. Though the black-and-white photograph was fuzzy, the marks on the person's neck sent a chill down the Chief's back. "They look like bite marks. You can see for yourself. The bodies are at the morgue."

Mooney stared at the officer for a second, then took a slow, deep breath and formed the words, "I want to look at these bite marks with my own eyes."

Mooney's Model T arrived at the morgue on Saint Philip Street just as the sun crept below the horizon. Mooney would speak to the coroner and investigate the strange murders himself, instead of listening to a bunch of nonsense from the men he supervised. A madman reigning terror on the French Quarter with an axe was one thing. A wild animal killing people by draining their blood was something he dreaded having to address to the public.

The morgue was cold like an underground cave, the smell of thiol causing his breath to catch in his throat. The coroner, a tall, thin man in his middle years, had as cold a personality as the building he presided over.

"Hey, Doc. What do you think was the cause of death?" Mooney didn't waste any time getting to the business at hand.

The doctor squinted at the pages on the clipboard he held. "Well, I'm not one hundred percent yet, Chief, but I've narrowed it down to a few possibilities. I don't think an animal could have done this, because I've never seen a specimen with fangs that match the bite marks on the victim's necks. I'm also not aware of any animal that can suck a person's blood completely from their body. If I had to say animal, maybe a large cat, but the bite marks are too...too..."

"Too what?"

"Too *narrow*." Doc looked frustrated and tired, his bald head shining with sweat. This many bodies made for long days.

"What do you mean, they're too narrow?" Mooney squinted at the coroner, intent on finding an answer. Narrow teeth didn't make sense in this context.

"Take a look and you'll see." The coroner walked over to a mortuary coffer, released the latch and rolled out a long steel drawer. A lifeless body, a young woman in her late twenties, skin as pale white as the granite walls, lay naked, covered only with a sheet. The coroner touched the dead woman's head with gentle hands, turning her to one side and brushing locks of dark brown hair away from her face and neck, revealing two perfectly placed intrusions.

Mooney focused on the wounds, his heart sinking. What he stared at made his head spin. *This was no animal.* For a short instant, he almost wished it had been the Axeman. *At least the Axeman had a rationale.* The precise punctures on the woman's neck had sucked all the veracity out of the room; two dark little holes stared Mooney square in his face and laughed at whatever worldview he'd formed up until that moment, mocking Mooney's understanding of reason and sense.

He sucked in a breath, holding it for a long moment. "What do you think caused this?"

The coroner shook his head. "Again, I'm not certain. My assistants looked at this. I even called a physician who works out of Touro infirmary. Even he's at a loss. My best guess is... an animal. But—"

His words hung in the air like smoke from a fire, tarnishing Mooney's perception of reality.

"But what, Doc?"

Tilting the woman's head back to its original position, the doctor pulled the sheet back over her body. "An animal we've never identified. The fangs that could've done this are not like anything I've ever seen."

"How are you certain they're bite marks and not something caused by a weapon?"

"I can tell the difference," the other man said, his tone neutral. "This was carried out by something living. The side of her neck is bruised and swollen where the mouth was pressed to draw out the woman's blood."

Mooney nodded, hoping he hadn't offended the doctor. "We appreciate your time, Doc."

"Sure. Would you like to see anything else? Perhaps another body?"

"No, I've seen what I needed to see," he said. "We'll be in touch if we need anything else." Mooney looked at the two perfect holes one last time. He ran his hand through his still-damp hair and put his police cap back on.

———

Colette, Jermain, and their father, Charles Dupré, lived in a small studio apartment on Ursulines Avenue between Henriette Delille Street and Treme Street. The trio had lucked out with their current living situation. Jermain met their landlord a few years prior at a pub that hosted vampires. Around this time, there were ordinary citizens who thought it chic to play dress up and pretend to be vampires. Their landlord, Guy Deano, a portly Sicilian man, was present at the meetup—he was the landlord of the pub.

Jermain had noticed a flyer for apartments available for rent. Guy took a liking to Jermain, who'd always been a smooth talker, charming and handsome. He'd also taken a liking to Colette, but she'd said she felt he stared at her for too long—long enough to make her feel uncomfortable.

It was hard for them to find a place to live. Their father was ill, unable to move or care for himself, and didn't speak much. He was barely awake for any prolonged amount of time. Usually, he'd wake up to have a small amount of blood they'd bring him, and then, he'd go right back to sleep after feeding. Colette and Jermain decided it was best to keep him hidden, their little secret. Mr. Dupré had grown pale and lost most of his body mass. He was all bone and the sight of him would have scared even the vampire club crowd.

Their father never complained to his children but, after he'd been turned, it seemed he never fully recovered from his wounds. Colette and Jermain, on the other hand, had become noticeably stronger after they'd been fully turned into vampires. All of their senses, their sight, hearing, smell, taste, had become increasingly sharpened. Their father's health, on the other hand, had turned for the worse. He would not accompany them on their hunts. More recently, his appetite had dwindled and he barely touched his suste-nance, despite Colette promising him the human's blood she'd brought him was exceptionally appetizing.

It was late spring, the trees flush with tiny, fragrant blooms, and Colette ambled along Frenchman Street, just past Chartres. The sun was down; candles and lanterns were lit outside the parlors and cabarets. The smell of raw sewage was pervasive, but she carried a perfumed fan to chase it away. The pulse of jazz emanated from venues as she sauntered past drunkards, whores, and heathens in her heavy, black cloak. Even after Mardi Gras had come and gone, plenty of people continued to dress in costumes and wear masks. Colette camouflaged seamlessly with the Voodoo practitioners, occult enthusiasts, hoodlums, and vampire copycats who roamed the streets late into the night.

The waning crescent moon sketched shadows across the pavement, and the sounds of piano keys and chords rever-berated through tavern walls, reminding her of her youth. Colette was hungry, but she'd gotten into an argument with her brother earlier and didn't feel like hunting. Jermain had grown increasingly paranoid and scolded her because he thought she'd been preying on too many aristocrats of late. She'd discovered during their argument that he'd withheld some information from her. He'd seen a few men in ulster coats following them throughout the Quarter for several weeks.

"The police are going to find us," he'd said, frowning.

She hated when her brother scolded her. It made her so angry and upset she cried, a red rainstorm erupting from her eyes. Every time she cried, blood poured out. She'd never seen another vampire cry, so she didn't know if they also cried blood. Perhaps it was only her who'd been cursed with such an unfortunate disorder. She didn't understand why her father and brother never cried. *Were they always this affectless? Another dress ruined*, she thought.

Jermain's words kept running through her head. "If you keep it up, Cole, they're going to find out where we live and they'll find Father. It'll be difficult for us to get away. Why can't you just do as I tell you?"

Her brother had decided to take the reins when they'd all turned. It was an unspoken agreement that, since their father was feeble and unable to guard over them or take care of himself, Jermain acted as head of their household. Colette figured this arrangement worked at least until their father regained his health. They hadn't received any formal vampire training, but Jermain seemed to have the best grasp of what they'd become.

"We must only stalk the night from approximately one thirty in the morning until four in the morning. Any time outside of those parameters, our chances of getting caught grow tenfold," Jermain said.

"How would they catch us? We're much faster." Colette enjoyed testing the limits of her nascent powers. She learned just one week after first being turned that she had about a seven-foot vertical jump. After a few weeks of practice, she'd managed to increase it to ten feet. Her brother, who was seven inches taller than her, got about twelve to thirteen feet. Not only did he have an impressive vertical, he could also levitate for a few seconds. She'd see him practicing his levitation skills in their backyard several times a week.

She also speculated she could read some humans' minds. She wasn't entirely sure, though.

"Do you think we can read minds, Jermain?"

He tilted his head, as if considering her question, before responding, "I'm not sure."

"Have you felt anything? Last time we brought the man home for Father, I could've sworn I heard his thoughts." She stared at her brother, gauging his reaction. "You didn't hear any of his thoughts?"

"I was too busy preparing him for Father. I wasn't trying to listen to anybody's thoughts," Jermain said, rolling his eyes.

Colette ventured off that evening without telling Jermain. A break from one another would do them good. Father was asleep. He slept often and they allowed him to, hoping he would get better. Bats were known to sleep for twenty hours or more throughout the day. Father had them outclassed if there were ever a sleeping competition. Some days, he didn't even wake up to feed.

The warm, round tones of a jazz piano echoed around her, and Colette stared down at the cobblestones, a dour expression on her face as she promenaded along Frenchmen Street. A horse and carriage galloped past, carrying an old wealthy couple. It made her remember when their family had their own coachmen and they traveled around the French Quarter and neighboring towns in a luxurious carriage. They would ride out to their parents' friends' plantations in Destrehan and even Darrow, which was an all-day ride. She would enjoy gazing at the scenery when they rode. The cypress trees draped in Spanish moss; the mighty Mississippi; the charming riverfront towns. Forced to live in the shadows, they were now deprived of their former comforts and had very little in terms of possessions. She acted uppity around her brother and father to maintain positivity, but often, her thoughts were overtaken by a dark tide of sorrow and despair.

Colette's thoughts returned to the argument she'd had with her brother. It had been fifty-one years since they'd been turned into vampires. It was now the year 1919 and, after every passing day, Colette wished she could go back in time. She wanted to travel back to the Shrove Tuesday evening of 1868, save her mother and defeat the evil vampire before he ravaged her family. They'd had a nearly perfect life. She would have found a suitor, she thought, and eventually married and had children of her own. *Mother and father would have loved grandchildren.*

She was sure Jermain would have found a lovely woman to marry and have a family of his own. They'd been members of the New Orleans aristocracy, after all, and would have married well. She felt tears coming again, and tried with all her might to suppress them. If someone were to see her, she didn't want to explain why her face was covered with blood. If it were to get to that point, she'd have to kill them.

As she walked along the Quarter, Colette's thoughts seethed like a caldron, slipping from her deep past to the present. A thick lump formed in her throat, her head down as she dawdled along, counting the stones on the street.

A small boy sat in the alley, back against the wall, knees pulled up to his chest. He looked to be no more than eight or nine. Children would oftentimes be out in the Quarter during the night. Many played an instrument, usually a cornet or a drum, trying to collect coins from passersby. But this child seemed odd. He held no instrument and, from where Colette stood, his posture looked sullen, accompanied by heavy breathing. He wore an oversized cloak and, every few seconds, he whimpered. His face was turned away from her, short dark hair curling against a fragile neck.

Colette looked around to see if he was part of a group,

but there weren't many others out. People were still inside the pubs, gambling dens, and jazz lounges, but not a single soul traversed Frenchman Street besides her and the child. She turned into the alley and started towards the boy.

"Hello. Why are you out here all by yourself?" she asked. "Little boy?"

Colette didn't prey on children. It was a rule she and her brother agreed upon, that they would not harm anyone under the age of fifteen. Still, she worried about the boy. *Why was he out so late by himself?*

She raised her voice to make sure he heard her. "Little boy, are you okay?"

The young boy sprang up from the ground and bolted away from Colette. She followed after him, but stopped after a few steps. How odd that he'd run. He didn't even know what she was.

A lasso dropped over Colette's head and chest and tightened, clenching firm around her arms and body. *No!* She let out a high-pitched scream as a hood covered her head, then someone tied a sturdy rope around her feet. Needles pricked through her clothes and skin. There were several quick jabs—ten, possibly more. Firm hands picked her up and carried her as she struggled against her bonds, still screaming.

She wasn't sure how many assailants there were holding her, but there were at least two strong men, maybe more, with powerful grips. She squirmed and writhed about, attempting with all her might to break free from their clutch, to no avail. The drug they'd injected her with had begun to exert its influence. She heard a door open, and they transitioned from the alleyway into a building. She heard the door slam behind them, and then she felt more needles penetrate her arms, back, neck and legs.

Funny, she thought. *Usually, I'm the one doing the piercing and the stalking. Tonight, it seems I'm the prey.*

Colette's vision dimmed until her eyes closed underneath the hood, and her thoughts entered a dream.

Her mother's limbs strewn on a bed, helpless. The pianist aggressively entered her. She lay motionless, eyes wide, bewitched by his commanding spirit. His eyes grew large, his nose appeared pointier, his ears sharp, bat-like. His teeth... his teeth, *hideous*. Satan's teeth. Jagged, white fossils, somehow still showing hints of white despite their piercing and slicing through her mother's flesh.

"Mother!" Colette attempted to speak, but she was unable to produce a sound, a ghost in the room.

Her father arrived too late to save their mother—or them. If only he'd arrived a few minutes earlier, they might have survived. He'd tried to avenge them, even after his children had already been turned, even after their mother's death. He'd gotten bitten himself, but he wasn't like them, for some reason. Father had given up after that. The loss was too great for him to bear. True love lost can break even the strongest spirit.

Colette's eyes opened but, just as before, all she saw was black. She felt the hood still draped over her head. She sat on a chair, her hands tied behind her, fastened to the back of the chair with iron handcuffs. She tried to move. The pain surprised her. She hadn't felt such intense pain in fifty-one years. Something wasn't right.

The hood was lifted from her head and her eyes took a few moments to adjust to the change in lighting. She looked around, blinking, attempting to take in as many details as she could as quickly as possible. A reddish glow from the overhead bulb barely illuminated what appeared to be a room in a factory. She supposed it was a factory, since she spotted lofty ceilings and tall casement windows in the periphery of her vision.

"I wouldn't try to move much, if I were you," a man's voice, deep and detached, said from behind her.

A cloaked figure stepped around the chair and into her field of vision. It stood a good six feet away from her, obviously a man, wearing black gloves and holding a sharp spike in one hand. His large hood concealed his face.

"I suggest you don't move your arms or your feet. Unless you enjoy pain."

Colette shifted her eyes down and saw her feet were spiked to the wooden floor, a pair of oversized nails lodged through both tops of her feet, preventing her from escaping the chair. Blood oozed out of the holes. She realized they must have nailed her hands to the backside of the chair, because every miniscule movement caused her palms to burn with pain.

Nailed to a chair, she thought. Did the police finally catch her, as her brother had warned her? She'd let her defenses down for a moment and this was the price she would pay. *How the hell am I going to get myself out of this?*

"How long have I been here?" Colette asked, her voice weary and her throat rough from screaming.

She heard others in the room, breathing. They did not respond.

"What do you want from me," she asked, her tone cold so they wouldn't know the severity of her pain.

"Who are you? Who is that boy you travel around with? Is he your brother," the cloaked man asked. His voice held loathing.

The gears in her head were spinning. *Do they know*

where we live? All she could think about at that moment was her brother and father. If they were asking, they must not know where they were.

She stirred her hand and excruciating pain coursed through her bones, reminding her to hold her tongue before she answered.

"Maybe, instead, I should ask you, *what* are you? Because you clearly aren't human." The question held a bitter edge.

Colette smiled, then. "I'm the girl who's going to rip your heart out and eat it for breakfast."

"Toss me the whip." He exchanged the spike for a whip made of hard leather.

Murmurs filled the room, a stir of anticipation. She tried hard to read their thoughts. She closed her eyes and focused.

How is she not dead, one mind thought.

She focused on the man questioning her, attempting to garner any bit of useful information she could. She needed to know what they were thinking.

She's a demon... must be a possession. Another mind held revulsion, and fascination.

"I have to use the bathroom," she said.

"Just go where you're sitting, wretch. I've seen you attack people. I've been following you for some time. That young man you travel with, the one with the blonde hair is your brother, isn't he? Where did you all come from?" The man's voice was eager and angry all at once.

"I'll tell you if you let me pee," she said with a small sniffle, peering at him from beneath her lashes. "Please, mister. I'm going to pee my knickers."

The man swung the whip with a violent crack, and it ripped open a gash on Colette's forehead. She closed her eyes and sucked in the pain, focusing elsewhere so as to not allow herself to appear weak. Blood poured down her face.

He gave a cruel laugh. "We can do this all night, peach."

"Call me peach again and you'll wish I were a demon from hell." She spat blood on the man's cloak.

He looked down at the wetness on his cloak and lifted his hand again. He whipped her until she passed out, the pain unbearable.

When she woke, they'd tied oversized, heavy-duty chains around her and secured them to strong locks on the floor.

The next evening, they continued their inquisition, beginning the torture all over again. She said nothing, just endured. They beat her again, gave her more of the disorienting drug. After the second day and night, Colette lost track of time.

The smell of coffee infiltrated Colette's nostrils. She licked bloody lips. *How bad do I look?* she wondered, then smiled at the thought. *Who would care at this point?*

The ringleader, in his cloaked anonymity, raised the whip and, as he was about to unleash another lash at Colette's head, the whip stopped. Something caught the whip in mid-air and, in a blink, it was wrapped around her assailant's neck so tight, his head detached from his body in a spray of blood and gore. The men lurking in the darkness sprang forward and toppled over her, knocking her chair over, causing the nails to rip through both her feet. Right before she crashed to the floor, she caught a glimpse of her brother, his face splashed with blood and his lips pulled back in an almost animal snarl.

Jermain, she thought, relief like a salve to her wounds.

Men shrieked, loud groans and moans of pain filling the air as her brother ran through them like a skilled predator. She couldn't see much as she lay, still nailed to the chair, her head now pressed against the factory floor, but she heard her brother smash, impale, cut, and kill until he stood near her, breathing heavily.

"Are you okay?" He sounded exhausted.

"I'll live," she managed to say, though pain traveled throughout her body like electricity through a live wire.

Jermain carefully removed the large nails from her hands and set her free from the chair, helping her to her feet. Colette got up slowly and stretched, her body free for the first time in several days.

"How long have I been here?"

"Too long," Jermain said. "I'm sorry it took so long to find you."

Jermain investigated the men's pockets, searching for clues as to their identities, but the men weren't holding any belongings on their person. Upon searching the room, Jermain found a card inside a desk. *Private Investigator Joseph Gorman.*

"They were investigators. Someone must have hired them to track us down." Jermain showed Colette the card, but she couldn't even take it, given the damage to her hands.

"They saw us prey on people," she muttered, trying to remember what else they'd asked her. "They suspected we weren't human."

"Goddamnit." He took his handkerchief from his breast pocket and motioned her to give him her hands.

She knew he wanted to scold her for being careless. It was clear he'd have a more serious talk with her after she'd recovered. It wasn't the time to discuss her mistakes. He was probably right, she thought. She had, in fact, feasted on too many aristocrats in the Quarter and someone had noticed. The private investigator had asked her what she was. They knew she and her brother weren't human, but at least they didn't know about her father.

Did they think we were vampires? Who else knew about us? she wondered.

Back at their studio on Ursulines Avenue, Jermain packed the few belongings they had into a trunk and moved it to the hallway.

"What are you doing?" Colette's hands and feet were burning with pain, and she wasn't able to help him. She hobbled around the apartment, the gashes in her hands and feet deep. Dark blood welled out of the tops of her feet and both her hands, straight through gauze bandages Jermain had wrapped for her. They would heal, but it would take time. Since neither of them had been this badly mutilated before, Colette wondered if she'd have to carry scars after her wounds closed.

Jermain sighed, sounding irritated. He floundered with their belongings, stuffing the trunk full of clothing and personal items from their closet.

"You're going to be all right. You'll recover," he said.

Colette followed him around the living room. "Why are you packing?"

"We can't stay here," her brother said, still hurrying around the house. He didn't bother to fold or wrap anything. "Whoever hired the investigator probably knows where we live. We have to go. Tonight."

"Tonight?" Colette turned to look at the portieres that separated their father's living space, her heart racing. "Where are we gonna go?"

Jermain shook his head, not even bothering to look at her. "I don't know. We'll have to find some place, an abandoned warehouse or building somewhere."

"Jermain," she began, but Jermain cut her off, his voice impatient. "Help me get Father."

Despite her agonizing pain, Colette helped her father off his sunken coffin and explained to him they couldn't stay there any longer. Charles didn't resist nor ask any questions and let his daughter navigate him onto his feet. He walked slowly towards the front door. Jermain lugged the massive trunk over.

"What will we do about the cadavers," Colette asked, looking toward the back closet. She paced back and forth. Each step produced more pain than the last, but she was too restless to stand still. There were several bodies in the apartment they hadn't yet disposed of.

Her brother turned, still holding the trunk, and inspected her bleeding feet. "We're going to have to leave them. There's no time."

Banging rattled the front door, startling them both.

"POLICE! Open up!"

Jermain dropped the trunk and it crashed on the floor. The clothes he'd packed spilled out all over the floor.

"OPEN UP NOW OR WE'LL KNOCK THIS DOOR DOWN!"

Jermain whirled around and flew towards their father in a sweeping motion. Colette's eyes followed Jermain's supernatural movements, her mouth open and her jaw slacked in awe.

"Cole, come on," Jermain said, cradling their father in his arms like a baby, and crashed through the back window, glass shattering around them in a spray of prismed light. Colette looked back towards the front door as the hammering grew louder and more intense. She hesitated for an instant, then turned and ran towards the broken window.

The latches on the front door gave out and a policeman burst through and into the apartment. Colette looked back as he raised his revolver and aimed it at her as she attempted to wiggle through the window, and fired two shots. Fire burst through her, and she shrieked, falling through the apartment window to smash on the pavement below with a loud thump. She felt like every bone in her body was broken, as she lay there stunned.

"Ow!" Colette cried out.

She heard rustling in the apartment.

"Oh, my God, what the hell's that smell?" someone blurted from upstairs.

Then she heard the sounds of retching. Colette tried to lift herself from the pavement, but she couldn't move.

"Is that a coffin?" a shaky voice cried from above.

"My god, there's corpses in the closet!" another voice yelled.

In the yard, Colette lay panting, hands smeared with blood from the gut shots. As her life ebbed, her mortality screamed through her memories. Her mind traced back to the night she'd been turned in her old home, in their old dark cellar. She scarcely recalled her life as a human girl or what pain had felt like back then. Her life as a mortal seemed like nothing but a distant dream; she questioned whether she'd ever lived as a human girl or whether it was a life she'd imagined. *Am I actually feeling pain? How can I feel pain if I'm technically dead?*

———

Frank Mooney burst through the front door and, in an instant, the smell of rotting corpses smacked his face. He'd never smelled anything like this in his long career.

"Where'd they go?" No one answered, all struggling to compose themselves, nauseated from the stench. "Where?"

"They went out the back window," one of the officers replied, still bent at the waist, his arm trembling as he pointed to the back wall. "Roth shot the girl. Definite hits. She might still be out there."

Mooney headed towards the opening and peered out the second-floor window. What he saw seemed like something out of a nightmare or a horror movie. A young man, no more than sixteen or seventeen, swooped off the balcony of the house opposite where Mooney stood. The young man, face pale and white as stone, hair long and blonde hovered down to pick up a girl who lay inert and bloody on the ground. He lifted her up like a feather, and then leapt back on the roof of the house across the yard.

"What in the world?" Mooney muttered, glancing back at his officers behind him. "This can't be real."

The other officers hurried over to the window but, by the time they'd arrived, the blonde boy and girl were gone. The officer who shot Colette looked down, then stuck his head out the window and searched the ground below.

"Where'd she go?" he asked, his voice unsteady. "I shot her twice right in the back. She fell out the window."

"Gone," Mooney replied, shaking his head.

Chief of Police Frank Mooney never saw Colette, Jermain or their father, Charles Dupré, again. He tried searching for them for three months after the incident, but decided it was probably best he end his search. He'd almost had them.

After that unforgettable day, no one believed Mooney when he'd tell people what he'd seen. His officers laughed at him behind his back and began to call him a loon. Others simply gave him funny looks. He realized that whatever he was after was probably something he couldn't, or better yet, shouldn't solve.

The young man with the golden mane leaping off the second-story balcony, levitating down to scoop up the young girl, leaping back on top of the house, then disappearing replayed in Mooney's mind like a sinister dream. Mooney realized, if it wasn't just his imagination, it must have been the devil or a demon, and the paranormal, he'd decided, he wouldn't go near. He was due to retire in eighteen months, and he'd much prefer to live out the remainder of his days not chasing down a cursed spirit. When Detective Frank Mooney wrote his memoir, he considered including the incident of the flying demon. In the end, he'd decided not to include what he'd witnessed.

CHAPTER 7

THE LUMBER FACTORY

DARK GRAY CLOUDS hung over a factory building in the desolate Louisiana Plains. A sign at the entry gate declared it the A.T. Cromwell Lumber Factory.

Inside, piles of wood and equipment crowded a sawdust-covered floor and the back section held discards and empty boxes piled high. In a large empty storage room filled with mostly empty shelves, Charles wheezed: "There's a heavy storm coming." He looked frailer than ever, his cloak long and heavy over his bony frame. His eyes hid in the hollow orbits of his skull. "I can sense it," he said.

It was one of those rare occasions where Charles sat perched up in his coffin, discussing life and their plans on how to procure fresh, salubrious blood.

"Jermain, are we sure this dwelling is safe?" Charles asked, surveying their new shelter. The thick metal door covering the entrance of the storage room sported a new latch and industrial-looking padlock, and was almost invisible from the main factory floor unless you knew where to look.

"We're safe here," Jermain said, glancing over at his sister with a stiff smile.

Jermain wasn't sure whether they were or weren't safe, but he figured being far away from the populace meant there was less likelihood of being tracked by authorities. He also supposed it was better to assuage his father and sister's worries with comforting assurances. He'd gotten them out of perilous situations in the past and he would continue to protect them from harm moving forward.

Thunder cracked outside the lumber factory, muffled by the heavy industrial door. Jermain found the factory outside of the city on one of his journeys to map the city and its suburbs for possible escape routes. After fleeing their living quarters on Ursulines Avenue, he'd decided it would make a perfect refuge, at least while they planned their next move. The smell of dust and oily machinery pervaded their new living space, but he knew Colette preferred this to the raw sewage that blanketed the French Quarter. The factory they'd found appeared to be forgotten and hidden in a remote part of Louisiana. Now, the trio truly resided in the shadows.

Jermain nursed Colette's still-healing wounds with care after he'd rescued her, and they'd escaped the police assault on their apartment. He'd fed her his own blood, mainly because he was afraid to leave her alone (to go hunting) and also because of the storms.

Shortly upon settling in their new dwelling in August 1919, two storms hit, back-to-back. Colette was bed-ridden for ten days before she could walk again without feeling intense pain in her limbs and back. The holes in her hands and feet caused by the spikes took that long to close. Two weeks after she'd been shot, all that was left as a reminder were small concave craters, barely noticeable, just two small depressions only evident if one was up close or touched the area. He was happy for her that they hadn't left big, ugly scars.

The first storm that traveled through Louisiana when they first arrived at the lumber factory was catastrophic. It made landfall just as they took shelter, preventing Jermain from hunting for four days due to severe winds and heavy rainfall. Then, two weeks later, another storm hit. Since he'd been nursing both his father and Colette with his own blood and wasn't able to hunt for fresh meals, Jermain grew weary. On a few occasions he blacked out, only to be awoken by Colette's pleas for more blood.

The cellar was rectangular, twenty feet by twelve feet and well-suited for hiding, since it had an eight-foot wall, a divider of sorts, three quarters of the way in from the entrance that partitioned the room. Colette and Jermain managed to build a basic but functional coffin for their father and placed it on the other side of the wall. They'd gathered up some cotton, horsehair and wool to line Father's coffin, making it as comfortable as possible for him. The coffin was placed in such a way where it remained concealed in case anyone were to stumble into the room. There was a single electrical outlet, which they plugged a bare lightbulb into. Apart from some loose metal objects left behind from old factory equipment and wooden planks, the factory seemed that it had been forgotten.

During the day, they rested. At night Colette and her brother either roamed the factory floor freely or they would go out on hunts to make their hideout more comfortable.

———

One evening while wandering about the floor, Colette found a penny. 1920. Lincoln's profile on the front side of the coin. Colette liked pennies because she could hold them without being harmed. Silver coins, mainly dollar coins, hurt her hands since they were ninety percent pure silver.

"Jermain, look." She held the penny up to the candle's flame.

Jermain studied the penny. "Lincoln," he said. "Nice find."

Colette thought back to March, 1861, when Lincoln was elected President of the United States, and she was only eight years old. A young girl in love with ballet, music, and painting. At the time, she wasn't fully aware of all the political happenings manifesting between the North and the South, but she did hear the name Lincoln often. She'd heard her mother and father speak of him and how many of father's friends were not thrilled he was the newly elected president. She remembered hearing her father say something about how Lincoln had divided the country and went against what the South stood for. Charles supported John C. Breckinridge throughout the election of 1860. Colette didn't understand much of what she heard, but the famous names stuck with her throughout the years.

Colette formed a worldview that everything that mattered to the human race came down to three things: money, power, and greed. All the famous mortals she'd ever heard or read about had fought wars to satisfy their egos and gain more land, power and, ultimately, money and resources. It was endless greed; the desire to stroke one's ego. Looking at humanity through such a lens made it easier on her conscience to feed on people. *Not much different from what we've become*, she thought. Shifting her thoughts in these ways would assuage her guilt when she'd take a life.

Colette caressed the small concave hole on her stomach where a bullet had gone through. She found that rubbing the small craters sometimes felt soothing. They were like two additional belly buttons, she thought.

"Sometimes I don't feel bad that we feed on them," she said to her brother, as she massaged the sunken scar.

"And why is that?" Jermain asked.

"All they seem to do is kill each other anyway. I read in the Times-Picayune there were an estimated twenty to twenty-three million casualties during the Great War. That included civilians and military personnel. When you hear statistics like that, I guess you don't feel as bad when you have to prey on a few every now and then in order to live."

"That many humans died in the Great War, huh?" Jermain asked with an air of surprise.

Colette nodded, staring off into the distance. "They're calling it the bloodiest war ever. Worse than the War Between the States."

"That's a lot of wasted blood," Jermain said, lifting an eyebrow.

She laughed.

He smirked, then turned more serious. "Have you thought about your new name?"

"Yeah. I'm going to go by Jazzie," Colette said.

"You really dig jazz music, don't you?"

"No doubt about it," she said, snapping her fingers and shimmying. She began to swing her arms and move her feet. Jermain clapped as she danced a number.

"What's your new name going to be?" she asked.

"Seth."

Colette thought about it for a moment. "So dark. I like it!"

"Listen, Cole, there's something we need to talk about. I

know you like reading about history and you pass the time with your nose in books, but—" Jermain said, matter-of-factly.

Colette looked at him, noting his sudden seriousness. She couldn't remember when he stopped being a teenager and became an adult. He wasn't as fun as he used to be. But she followed his lead with little second guessing because, after all, he was the reason they were still alive fifty-some-odd years after having been turned. Jermain was the reason she and, more importantly, their father, was still around. So she listened and did as he instructed.

"What do you want to talk about?"

"We have a gift. I need you to practice more. I never see you practice your levitation or exercise your other physical abilities." His jaw tightened, his blue eyes fixed on her, cold and heavy. "I've been uncovering some other new abilities."

Colette perked up. "Yeah? Like what?"

"Well, I'm not one hundred percent on this yet, but I think I can translocate."

"You can do what?" Colette stared at her brother, eyes wide.

"Translocate. It means move between locations. I think I can do it." Jermain snapped his fingers. "I have to concentrate. I'm almost positive I've done it. It left me feeling dizzy and disoriented and I don't feel like trying it right this second. But I'll try it another time and you can watch. I want to make sure I'm not dreaming it up or imagining I've done it."

"That's remarkable!" She clapped her hands.

"We have gifts, baby sister. But we can't let them go to waste." Jermain glanced over at their father. "There's something else I wanted to speak to you about." Jermain's voice turned flat. He hesitated for a moment, then continued,

"Father is getting worse. I think he might die soon." He looked at her, his gaze solemn. "I've been trying to figure out why we're so strong and why father is—"

Colette could guess what her brother was getting at.

"Weak," she said.

Jermain shook his head. "It's more than that. It seems as if he's decaying slowly over time. Like a fruit decomposing—"

"Jermain..." Colette stroked her hair, a nervous habit. "Why do you think we were turned, but Mother wasn't? Why did Şerban kill her?"

"I don't know," he said with a sigh. "I haven't really thought about it. I've been more worried about why Father is in the condition he's in."

"What have you come up with?" Colette asked. He'd sparked her curiosity. She spent her energy caring for her father, but hadn't given too much thought to why hadn't he developed powers like they had?

"I've been thinking back to that night. The night we were all turned. The night Mother..." He rarely brought up their mother. The thought of their mother being mauled and mutilated by the vampire cast a cloud over them. All these years later, and the thought of their mother's death continued to dampen their spirits. "Why kill her?" Jermain's shoulders slumped. "I mean, I know we kill people, too, but not like that."

Thinking of her most recent experience, Colette said, "Maybe humans deserve to die."

He nodded. "But did Mother? We could still have her, if he'd turned her."

"What good did it do Father? He's useless." Colette covered her mouth as soon as the words left it, stricken by the words.

What was strange was they, now, participated in slaughtering people in similar ways. Perhaps they weren't as violent. Unless the mortals deserved it, of course. Still, it was uncomfortable for them to think about. Why hadn't their mother been turned into a vampire?

"Father was the last one to turn." Jermain went on. "I've mulled this over in my mind, Cole. Over and over again. And the thing I keep going back to—to explain what happened." She could almost see the figurative light bulb above his head. Something went wrong from the very beginning of their transformation. "I don't think Father drank enough of the vampire's blood," Jermain finally said. "And I think that's why Father is in such a frail state. We had to drink a lot more than he did. Don't you remember?"

How could she forget? The details of that night were tattooed on her brain and, in that moment, it all came rushing back to her. Shrove Tuesday. Their old house. The party. The pianist. The dark cellar. The agony they'd all endured.

Colette shook away the cold feeling. "You think that's why Father is so weak?"

"It's the only explanation I have. If that's the reason, maybe we could help him. Get him strong like us," Jermain said.

How are we going to help him? Colette thought. No one taught them how to live—how to function or survive— as vampires. What to do when things went wrong. They'd had to figure everything out for themselves, mostly through trial and error. And there had been a lot of errors. Like the time Colette almost died because she drank the blood of four people in one night, back in the early days, shortly after they'd been turned. They'd learned drinking the blood of one person in one sitting was all they needed. They'd also learned blood varied from human to human, ranging from higher to lesser quality, and even varying in potency.

It had become more difficult for Colette and Jermain to find their prey since they'd moved to a more remote part of Louisiana, far from the city. The lumber factory was perfect for hiding, but now they were isolated and had to travel to find suitable prey. What was once a strategy game, in Colette's view, had become drudgery. They'd sometimes have to travel eight, nine, ten or more miles in a given direction to find blood. Sometimes, they resorted to hunting animals, cows, horses, dogs, and even cats, because people had become a scarce commodity.

Jermain and Colette spent a whole night stealing a steel coffin from a cemetery several miles away, floating it down a channel in the Bayou, so their father could sleep in comfort. They created make-shift mattresses for themselves, stuffing straw and cotton into sheets and sewing them shut. Most of their efforts were focused at making sure their father lived to see another day.

"Next night that the weather permits, I'm going to venture out to find a mortal," Jermain said, as he and Colette were readying themselves for bed.

Colette felt a pang of hunger as she snuggled down on her mattress. It felt as though sharp blades were jabbing at her insides. She didn't voice her hunger to Jermain. She knew he must have felt a similar sensation. Her internal clock told her it would soon be dawn, and in another moment, she fell asleep.

CHAPTER 8

WALLACHIA

THE WINTER MORNING was cool when Jermain ventured off at dusk to find a human to bring back for him, his father, and Cole to feed upon. They hadn't fed on a human in some time. The storms had finally subsided and Jermain saw his opportunity to hunt. The punishing terrain of the Louisiana wetlands made it difficult to travel far distances. It was a Catch-22—perfect for hiding, but difficult to find and feed on people. They usually settled for large birds—pelicans, egrets, wild turkeys. They would sometimes hunt racoons, muskrats, snakes, and even alligators. The alligators were more challenging and it wasn't an animal they hunted often. As keen as their eyesight was in the dark, Colette and Jermain speculated the gators had even better eyesight at night.

The night sky was black velvet. A few stars pierced the night sky, but did nothing to illuminate Jermain's trail. He waded through the marshes, transitioning from tall grassy land to waist deep, muddy salt water. He hopped across tussocks when he could avoid the deep marsh waters. He couldn't avoid wading through the salty marshes entirely, though it was a perilous undertaking. Jermain flinched at the wild sounds in the wetlands. They gave him an eerie feeling. His eyes were perceptive, even in pitch black darkness (when he was well-nourished), but he couldn't fully sense what was underneath the water. His senses allowed him to monitor a radius of about fifteen feet in either direction, but only three to four feet below water. He had also learned that he wasn't a competent swimmer after he'd been turned into a vampire. His stomach churned. A feeling of overwhelming weariness took hold of him, since he hadn't had any blood in more than one week. Now, he was blind in the pitch-black murk. The last blood he'd tasted was from a bird and it hadn't been that appetizing. Neither of them had tasted human blood in over three weeks. A lack of proper nutrition hindered his supernatural abilities and stunted his powers. It was something he had figured out mainly from experiencing periods of prolonged hunger and malnourishment. Disappointment and defeat began to enter his mind as he waded through the silent, dark night somewhere in the swampy marshes of southern Louisiana.

A quick stir beneath him startled Jermain. He swam faster, kicking with all of his strength. Neck deep in water, Jermain was pulled under by something clamped on his leg. He felt himself being dragged deep and rolled over and over until dizziness overtook him and he blacked out.

———

One hour later, a swirling mass torpedoed down from the night sky into the water where Jermain had disappeared. The object made a loud swooshing splash. A few seconds later, a man wearing a black brocade coat rocketed up through the marsh water, holding an eleven-foot alligator.

The man held the gator in both arms like an Olympic athlete, and with incredible momentum, heaved the nearly six-hundred-pound gator twenty feet into the air. The alligator bellowed; the noise carried through the air like a whistling truck engine. It landed with a heavy thud on a patch of solid grass. The gator squirmed onto its back and attempted to waddle back into the marshy water, but it moved too slowly.

The man levitated over to the alligator and turned it on its back again, with little resistance, as if the gator was stunned. With one razor-sharp nail, the man sliced through the alligator's belly, opening its leathery skin with little effort to stick his arm deep inside, rummaging for a moment until he latched onto something and pulled hard. Jermain's head, torso, and legs erupted from the alligator's belly, covered in a soupy mixture of thick, pinkish-red gastric fluids and goo. He reeked and did not appear conscious.

———

Several minutes went by before Jermain awoke, confused. He removed thick slime from his eyes, and managed to open them wide, meeting the cloaked man's gaze. Jermain opened his mouth and in a desperate gasp, he inhaled all the air he could.

"I thought it was over..." Jermain said, coughing up fluid. "...for me."

"It might've been if I hadn't rescued you" The man who stood over Jermain had frosty blue eyes and long dark hair streaking water down his coat. In his middle or late forties, he reminded Jermain of a rich man who'd once visited their plantation with fine features and slender-fingered hands.

Jermain had never seen him before, but he felt a chord

of ... sameness, recognizing something about the way the man held himself, the way he smelled.

"You're a vampire, aren't you? Like me." Jermain said, wiping off his face.

"Like you?" The other man let out a laugh. "I am most definitely a vampire. That is true." He lifted his chin disdainfully. "But we are nothing alike."

"How did you find me?"

"I've been following you, your sister and your father for some time," the other vampire said. "You are hardly quiet."

"How long?" Jermain pressed, his voice shaky. His head was spinning and he felt nauseous.

"Since there were reports of a young blonde man galloping over rooftops in the Quarter." The vampire let out a short laugh, taking his coat off to shake some of the water from it. "I have no intention of harming you or your family." His eyes were cold.

Jermain tried to move his legs, but they felt like wood. He wasn't sure what to make of the vampire, but he couldn't move, so there wasn't much he could do otherwise.

The vampire continued: "There was much talk around the Quarter of a flying demon. Many people, including the police, put together that you and your sister were responsible for many murders in the city. It was a wise decision to leave when you did," the vampire continued. "Which way shall we go? I'll carry you."

"We have to go north." Jermain pointed in the direction from which he'd come. "My legs aren't working. I can't stand up."

The man slid his coat back on, slung Jermain on his back like a sack of potatoes and began slogging through the marshes in the direction of the lumber factory.

"You'll regain full use of your legs in due time. Your

problem is you swam underwater for a good while and swallowed much water. Vampire's shan't swim, young prince." He adjusted his hold and kept talking. "The lovely thing about being a vampire is it's so very difficult to die. Vampires who do die usually do so because they break simple rules. You've much to learn."

———

Back at the factory, Colette heard the door creak open and the sound of footsteps began to click across the floor. They didn't sound like her brother's footsteps.

"Jermain?" Colette asked, in a tight, shaky voice. She moved to turn on the light bulb, and heard something banging loudly down the stairs.

When Colette saw the man, she cowered towards the back of the room. The smell of rotten swamp invaded the room. The man had dragged the alligator back from the swamp along with Jermain, who was slung over his right shoulder.

"Who is this, Jermain?" she said, her voice trembling.

Her brother craned his neck to look at her, then at the stranger. "This is—would you like to introduce yourself?"

"I am Alexandru," the other vampire said, straightening under the weight of his burden. "You don't have to be afraid of me, young lady. I am here to help you and your father. I saved your brother. I, too, am a vampire."

Colette's eyes panned from Alexandru to Jermain, looking for reassurance.

"A vampire? Like us?" she asked, noticing a coat of arms on the vampire's cloak. Its design was a crescent moon and a six-pointed star. The right side of the design featured six stripes.

"Yes, my dear." He flashed his fangs.

Colette gasped. "There are others..." she said, as if speaking to herself. "When were you... *turned?*"

"That is a long story." He hoisted Jermain upright and sat him on a wooden bench against the far wall. "I have been wandering the earth much longer than you, your brother, and your father, dear."

"There's a wheelchair over there," Jermain said, pointing to it in the corner. "We use it for father at times. Would you mind?"

Alexandru wheeled it over and hoisted Jermain onto it as if handling a doll.

Colette stared at Alexandru, her lips pursed.

Alexandru stared back at her. She felt his penetrating stare. Her hand moved up to her necklace, and she caressed it protectively.

"Are there many other vampires?" Colette asked. "You're the first we've met."

"There are some. Mostly in Europe. Not many in the New World—the Americas. We are a small tribe," Alexandru said. "Our race is very selective when deciding to convert a human."

Colette wondered how old Alexandru was. He appeared physically older than her and her brother, but he didn't look older than their father. She realized their age, at least their human age, didn't really matter when it came to vampire age. Though she still looked like she was sixteen, she was now sixty-eight years old. *God, I'm ancient*, Colette thought.

Alexandru pulled the alligator towards the center of the cellar. "For you and your father," Alexandru said, pointing to the gator, its oozing belly splayed like a science project.

"Jermain, are you going to have some, too?" she asked, moving toward the animal.

Jermain nodded, still lapped in the glutinous liquid from when the gator had ingested him.

"What is that all over you?" Colette said, grimacing as she studied the gooey substance dripping from her brother's face. She brought him a rag and helped him wipe it off.

Jermain pointed to the alligator. "This thing almost ate me. Well, it did, but Alexandru saved me in time. Let's drink. I'm hungry," Jermain said.

Colette drank the alligator's blood, then made her way over to her father, who lay still in his coffin. It was tasty, she admitted. Everything tougher to kill, for some reason or another, had a more savory flavor. She pried open Charles' mouth and allowed the alligator blood to cascade from her mouth into her father's.

"Father, we have a visitor," Jermain said.

Despite all the noise they'd made, Charles hadn't stirred since Jermain had returned, until Colette began feeding him.

While they fed, the enigmatic Alexandru began to speak.

"I knew Şerban well before he was invited to your old home," Alexandru said.

The name made the tiny hairs on the back of Colette's neck perk up.

"How do you know about him?" Colette asked.

She hated Şerban, loathed hearing his name. It felt strange to hear someone else say it out loud. Şerban. The vampire who'd ruined her family and her life. If she could kill him all over again, she would. The vampire had cursed her and her family to a hell where the raison de vivre was dictated by an eternal hunger for blood. Her face flushed red and her body heat increased to seventy-seven degrees Fahrenheit—ten degrees above her normal body temperature. Şerban was the vampire who'd left their father a shell, a shadow of the man he was when he was human. That pianist had left her and Jermain with the impossible burden of caring for their father, she thought. Caretakers of the damned and the eternal hunger.

"I had known him since the old country," Alexandru continued. His bright blue eyes blazed in the dark cellar. A few candles and the bulb struggled to illuminate their dingy space.

"Old country?" Colette eyed Alexandru suspiciously. *What does this vampire want from us? Why did he show himself now?* Colette's mind raced with paranoid thoughts.

"I am from Romania. As was Şerban. Your brother told me he turned you." Alexandru sighed, his accent deepening. "I was there from the beginning."

"No need to be cryptic." Jermain sounded sarcastic as he went on. "Be straight with us. We want to know everything."

Colette's back straightened. She was growing apprehensive with their new guest. *Maybe this Alexandru is not someone we should trust.* Vampire or not, she didn't like that he had old ties with Şerban. But they didn't know much about him, the history of their affliction. They needed information. Help and guidance, even. Just maybe not from him.

"Very well, then. I will attempt to be more direct with you. After all, you, your sister and your ailing father must have many questions." Alexandru motioned to Charles, who lay pale and lifeless in his coffin. He was deep in his slumber again after feeding, still unaware of Alexandru's arrival.

Alexandru's eyes locked with Colette's. They turned from frosty blue to obsidian black.

"The beginning," Alexandru said, his voice grave. "I was serving under Vlad III. I was a commander under his leadership in 1460 and led his army. This was during the bloody Turkish Wars. The Ottoman Empire ruled much of our lands back then. We fought the Ottomans several times to defend Wallachia."

"Vlad the Impaler," Jermain said. "Dracula."

Alexandru nodded, his dark hair brushing his collar. "Yes, that is the nickname he was given. His history—my history is not a Bram Stoker novel. He was and is still a hero in our homeland. The wars, the hordes of dead men, women, and children; the torture, his imprisonment. Over time, these travails made him lose his mind."

Alexandru's sharp, long nails tapped on the metal bench as he spoke, the grating sound of his nails sending a chill down Colette's back. There was something eerily familiar about his nails—about his hands.

"Vlad suffered greatly in the hands of the Ottomans. The things they did to him when he was captured. Bound and tortured in an underground prison. It's a miracle he was able to get out." Alexandru lifted his chin. "Doamne."

"Doamne?" Jermain asked. "Is that Romanian?"

"Lord. *Master*," Alexandru replied.

A suffocating silence swept the room. Colette yearned to know more. The gears in her head were spinning.

"How does Şerban tie into all this?" Jermain asked. "Who was he?"

Alexandru looked at him, his expression neutral. "I'll get to him shortly. You must know some of the history before we get to Şerban. Otherwise, nothing I say will make sense and it will sound like puzzle pieces scattered about randomly."

"Were you and Şerban friends?" Colette asked, her face hot.

"We were more than friends," the vampire said. "We were comrades. We commanded armies together. We helped Vlad escape from prison. We regained control of Wallachia and protected it against the Turks over and over again. Death and suffering." Alexandru looked at them with a clenched half-smile. "I do not wish to offend you," he went on. "But what you might consider suffering and torment is nothing compared to what I have witnessed. To what I have lived through."

Colette glared at the vampire, her eyes narrowed, her skin flushed and her back tensed. She didn't like being patronized.

"There was no mercy. We were instructed to cut off their heads... cut off the Turks' heads and impale them onto spikes. A head on a spike was a loud statement. It deterred our enemies and made them think twice before planning to attack our city." Alexandru seemed lost in his thoughts as he reminisced about days from long ago.

Colette watched him, then cleared her throat as the silence lengthened.

"Şerban was a powerful man...And even more powerful as a vampire." Alexandru's eyes narrowed. "Did you kill Şerban?"

Palpable tension struck the room, making Colette's skin tingle. She took a moment before answering.

"We did." She kept her voice as calm and even as she could.

His pale eyes focused on her, his gaze intent. "Are you sure? How do you know he was dead?"

Colette looked at her brother, trying to keep from looking nervous. She hoped Jermain would offer her reassurance.

Jermain said nothing.

Colette's heart didn't beat any longer, but she'd felt, in that tense moment, as if it were pounding in her chest. There was another time when she'd felt her heart had come back to life with a pulse or two, or even maybe, a pulse and a half. The time she was shot by the police. The beat was akin to a bomb detonating in her chest. She didn't like the sudden change in her system.

"Our father shot it right after it had attacked us," she explained. "Then I blasted it, too. We killed it." Colette's eyes met Jermain's. "Right, Jermain?" Her focus returned to her heart. *Is it beating? Was it her imagination?*

Alexandru studied Colette carefully. *Did he notice the uptick in my heartbeat?* she wondered.

Alexandru scoffed. "Shot him, you say? With a pretty little pistol? You're certain he's dead?"

Colette brought her hand up to her chest. *Did it beat again?*

Jermain cleared his throat. "We shot it several times with a powerful musket rifle. It wasn't a dainty little pistol. We saw it die," Jermain added. "Then our neighbor's staff stuffed its remains in the furnace and burned it."

Colette was reminded of the putrescent odor that assaulted them after Mrs. King and the help burned Şerban's remains in the cellar. The memories of the suffocating smell, their painful turning into vampires, and losing everything, came rushing back to her.

"Why do you refer to Şerban as it?" The other vampire looked truly perplexed. "Do you not realize that you are here, in fine fettle, thanks to him? Do you not see you are the same being as he was? You should be grateful for the gift he imparted on you."

"He ruined my family. I don't want to live like this anymore!" Colette cried, then broke out in tears. She sat on the ground, head and arms pushed towards her knees, crying blood on her plaid print dress. "We had a perfect life and he took it all away. He killed our mother. I'd kill him all over again if I could." Colette lifted her head, a scarlet river coating her cheeks with tears.

Jermain pushed himself over in the wheelchair towards Colette and pulled her up to put his arm around her. "Keep it together. Please, try to be strong."

Jermain turned to Alexandru. "We're certain Şerban is dead. We saw him burn."

"It is difficult to kill a vampire as old and powerful as Şerban," Alexandru said, a wry smile forming on his pale face. "Perhaps he isn't dead. He may still be wandering the earth and he may not be happy with what you've done to him."

"Listen, I appreciate you saving my brother from the alligator," Colette said, her voice cold. "But if you are really trying to help us, let's stop talking about Şerban and turn to the subject of our father's health."

Jermain and Alexandru turned towards the coffin where Charles lay in a deep slumber.

"Why is he weak? How come he doesn't have the same powers and vigor my sister and I have?" Jermain asked.

Alexandru sneered. "That is obvious. Your father did not drink enough of Şerban's blood. Do you remember the night clearly, when Şerban turned you?"

"Every second of it," Jermain said.

"Why did he kill our mother? Why didn't he turn her?" Colette asked, her voice choked.

"I'm sure Şerban had his reasons...but I cannot guess what they were, my lady." Alexandru rubbed his brow. "How much of Şerban's blood did your father take?"

"I don't think he took much at all," Jermain said. "Everything moved so fast."

Alexandru's words made perfect sense. Their father had shot Şerban before the vampire gave him blood. Their father, then, must have ingested just a small amount of the vampire's blood during their skirmish, or at some point before Şerban was killed.

"Hmm... He must have had *some* of Şerban's blood," the other vampire said, his brow furrowed. "Otherwise, he would not have been turned."

"If he did, then he only had a very small amount," Colette said. "Possibly when they were struggling, just before father shot Şerban."

"There lies your problem. You and your brother," Alexandru motioned towards Jermain, "most likely had a healthy dose of Şerban's blood. Your father, on the other hand, did not. There are two ways to help your father, and it will not be easy. Perhaps with some diligence, persistence and luck, you may succeed."

"How do we help him? What do we have to do?" Jermain asked, caressing his sister's back.

"One option is you hope Şerban is still alive and convince him to allow your father to drink more of his blood."

Impossible, Colette thought.

"I can't believe what I'm hearing. We killed that nauseating vampire," she cried out, unable to help herself.

"If that is the case, then you do have one other option," Alexandru said, deep in thought, as his chin rested on his fist. "You must find blood from a saint or from the descendent of a saint and feed it to your father. Only then will your father find his vigor and savor life as a fully formed vampire."

"A saint?" Jermain asked, his tone incredulous. "Saints exist?"

"Unfortunately, they do."

Colette sniffled, but needed to know more. "Why a saint's blood? Can't anything else help our father?"

Alexandru rubbed the back of his neck. "Listen to me. Nothing else besides what I've told you will work. This is not an easy undertaking. I have only encountered saints less than a handful of times, once during the Thirteen Year's War. We faced an army led by Prince Casimir of Poland, son of King Casimir IV. Our armies faced off in 1464." Alexandru closed his eyes. "Casimir's chain mail seemed to have a forcefield of protection, where any sword or weapon that struck it was deflected, as if by witchery or magic. Prince Casimir had God's protection, long before anyone knew he'd become a saint. The prince's sword was flawless; an extraordinary weapon that easily cut through men and horses like a hot knife slices through butter. His swiftness, his accuracy was a wonder I had never witnessed until then." Alexandru tapped his fingertips. "Prince Casimir was a powerful warrior with divine assistance. Our army lost those battles in the end, and the prince was able to hold steadfast to his lands. One of our soldiers managed to procure a small amount of his blood, which was used to nurse an ailing vampire back to life."

"I can't believe this. Saint blood. Where in the world are we going to find a saint? Before tonight, we had no idea there were any other vampires. Now, we find out there are saints." Jermain let out a heavy sigh. "Are there any other options to help our father?"

"I'm afraid there are not," Alexandru said.

Colette cried more blood, disappointed and saddened by Alexandru's words. Jermain sat on the wheelchair holding his head in his hands. Mr. Dupré rested quietly in his coffin. He hadn't stirred the slightest—remaining in a deep drowse—as the news was broken to his children.

Colette clutched her necklace, the necklace her uncle had given her. Technically, he'd gifted it to her mother, who then gave it to her. She began to pray. Her hand began to steam as if she'd touched a scorching hot iron. Her eyes released puffs of steam clouds like a train's blast pipe and her face turned blood red.

"Are you praying?" Alexandru asked, his voice filled with anger and frustration.

Billows of steam emanated from Colette's face.

"You cannot and shall not ever pray! You will die doing so! Do you not realize you are not welcome anymore in His eyes?" Alexandru pointed upwards. "You are a damned soul, restricted from ever receiving salvation in heaven."

Alexandru pointed at each of them, including himself, and then yelled, "We can never pray! It is against our nature."

"Take it easy. She's just scared, all right?" Jermain took hold of a nearby cloth and wiped away Colette's red tears. "We didn't even know there were other vampires besides us before tonight." Jermain lowered his voice, his arm draped over Colette's shoulder. "I mean, I'd suspected there were. I may have crossed paths with a few in New Orleans, but they didn't seem too friendly, like they were trying to avoid us and not get involved with our... *plight*. We're just looking for some answers and some help."

Alexandru's gaze settled on the ground.

"I didn't choose to be this way," Colette said, her voice choking between cries.

"You know, the more you cry, the hungrier you'll get. All you're doing is losing blood, which you'll have to replenish sooner rather than later," Alexandru said, his head still down.

They all fell silent.

"I'm certain we killed Şerban. So, where do we find a saint?" Jermain asked.

"That's an age-old question, child. You must look very hard. An alternative might be to find a descendent of a saint and get blood from them. If a person's lineage ties back to that of a saint's, there is a likelihood their blood can contain what your father needs to get better."

Colette realized Alexandru held the key to vampire knowledge, so they needed him, especially if he could save their father. He had knowledge of vampires and what they needed to thrive. She wished they'd crossed paths with him years ago, closer to that fateful night in 1868. Despite still having many questions and now ridden with even more anxiety, she knew the night would soon turn to dawn and they'd all had a long, tiresome evening.

"It will be dawn soon," Colette said.

"We really appreciate your advice and help. I give you my thanks, once again, for saving me from the alligator." Jermain rubbed his temples. "We're going to get some rest now. Thank you for everything. Do you have somewhere to stay? Somewhere you can go for the day?"

"You are right," Alexandru said. "It has been an eventful evening. Unfortunately, at this hour, I will not make it safely indoors to another dwelling before the sun rises."

Oh, my god, Colette thought. *You're not going to invite him to spend the day here, are you?*

Alexandru looked around their pitiful space. "May I stay here?

Jermain seemed to be debating whether to allow Alexandru to spend the day with them.

No, please. Say no. Colette tried to make eye contact, but Jermain avoided her gaze.

"Okay. You can spend the day. Do you need a mattress to sleep on?"

"That is not necessary. I will sleep on the floor."

"Are you sure?" Jermain asked.

After all these years, he hasn't forgotten his manners from his upbringing, Colette thought. Still, she didn't like this one bit. There was something suspicious about Alexandru. Why had he appeared to them just now after he admittedly spied on them for some time. Something wasn't right.

"Yes, you are very kind. I will be fine on the floor," Alexandru assured him, rising to remove his overcoat and lay it on the floor near the doorway.

"All right. Goodnight, Alexandru," Jermain said.

"Goodnight, Jermain." The other vampire looked over at Colette and smiled, flashing fangs. "Goodnight, young princess."

Colette didn't respond. She curled herself in a fetal position on her makeshift mattress and forced herself to go to sleep. She was tired of crying and wary of their new guest. She hoped he'd leave first thing at sunset the following day.

———

Colette woke to a shrill and unsettling howling. The screams sounded like Jermain's, though muffled. The room was a tomb of darkness, a silent and suffocating space that extinguished all light and sound. It was *too* dark, causing her to panic.

"Jermain? Are you all right?" her voice faltered.

She tried to rise and slammed her head into a solid surface.

"Ah, fuck!"

She reached up and felt a hard surface that extended around her like a box. Her back lay on a soft and plush material. The sides had soft padding, and she felt like she had no room to move. A coffin. *Father's coffin?* It was her only guess. *What the hell? How'd I get in here?*

Colette slammed her fist against the surface with all her might. Pain shot through her fist like snake venom. Something heavy had been placed on top to prevent her from getting out. She pressed her feet against the cover and attempted to kick it off. The cover wouldn't budge. She realized it would take a lot more force to break out. *I wish I had my brother's strength.*

Colette was used to the darkness. She'd spent her days with her brother and her father, mostly hiding in the shadows. The darkness now swallowed her hope as desperation filled her thoughts. *Am I going to die in this coffin?* She closed her eyes. She preferred to experience the blackness of her mind than the foreboding tenebrosity and claustrophobia the coffin instilled. She felt her neck. Something was missing. *Oh, no!* Her necklace was gone. Colette took a short, shallow breath and felt incredibly weak for the first time in a very, very long time.

Through the confines of the coffin, she continued to hear

clamoring. They were the faint sounds of struggle intermixed with her brother's piercing cries. The coffin and whatever had been placed on top dampened the sounds of struggle emanating from nearby, just past the partitioned wall. *I hope they're okay*, she thought, trying to calm her racing thoughts. Alexandru must have placed her in the coffin. She had a feeling he couldn't be trusted and now she could only hope her brother and father could get out of whatever plight they'd found themselves in. *Jermain, you're crafty and you'll think of something.*

———

Jermain heard a loud bang. His eyes opened and his fangs protruded. Springing up from his mattress, he saw Alexandru moving in the dark. He glanced down and saw his father groveling on the floor, out of his coffin. Jermain pinpointed Alexandru's location and attacked him with all his energy. They rolled on the floor, Alexandru's nails raking through Jermain's coveralls, tearing into his chest, arms, and mid-section.

Jermain attempted to block Alexandru's hands, rolling to the left, then the right, but Alexandru's attacks were lightning quick, and he made contact with his razor-sharp nails. In just seconds, Jermain had suffered a series of deep scratches all over his face and upper body. Jermain spun and managed to get up and onto his feet again for a brief moment, only to suffer more powerful blows that landed like mortars falling from the sky.

Jermain's legs now worked, but they still felt unsteady. Alexandru's fists felt like anvils smashing down on the young vampire's body, and Jermain's knees buckled. He was covered in his own gore and could scarcely see, as his eyes became clouded by the blood streaming from the gashes on his face.

Alexandru pinned Jermain's neck with his left arm, then smashed at Jermain's head with his right fist. Jolts of pain shot through the young vampire's head. The mature vampire's dominance terrified him. Jermain spit blood, some of it landing on Alexandru's face, only angering the old vampire. The Romanian vampire's fists came down harder on Jermain—his assault, a barrage of unrelenting blows, turned Jermain's face into a purplish-reddish pulp. His face was an almost unrecognizable, inflamed oval mass as he glimpsed his reflection on a small copper mirror.

Jermain felt a wire (galvanized wire?) wrap around his neck, and it squeezed tightly drawing blood. He writhed, his fingers sliding underneath the wire, attempting to lessen the pressure. The wire cut into his neck and sliced his fingers.

Pain and shock coursed through Jermain's flesh. Alexandru's choking grip was tight, vice-like, causing Jermain's eyes to bulge. The old vampire's grip tightened around his throat. It felt as if any additional pressure were applied, Jermain's head would surely snap off. He bit at Alexandru's hands; his fangs were his only weapon to fend off the nefarious enemy. Jermain clenched Alexandru's hands and pulled them apart just enough to alleviate the choking pressure.

While holding down Jermain, Alexandru took out a steel file from his cloak pocket and pressed it to Jermain's fangs, grating them, filing them down violently. The irregular scraping sound of metal on bone—the vicious back and forth of the file—made Jermain shake uncontrollably.

"Ah-hhhhh! Fuck!" Jermain yelped, as blood spattered from his mouth.

Alexandru sawed at one side and then the other like a deranged tooth surgeon. Blood sprayed in all directions. Jermain screamed like a feral animal caught in a deadly trap. He scratched and tore at Alexandru's head to stop him, but his attempts were fruitless. The old vampire was much more powerful and straddled him in a way that allowed him full control over the assault. Once he grew tired of sawing at Jermain's fangs, he continued smashing him with his fists, then used his hard, sharp elbows to strike Jermain's face. After a long stretch of throwing elbows, he switched again to the metal file, sawing away at the young vampire's fangs.

Jermain always thought he could live forever. He'd been developing his powers, growing more powerful as a vampire over the years. His mind-reading skills had improved. He levitated with more precision and control. In the midst of being marred and mauled by Alexandru, he saw all of that vanishing. The thought of whether his soul would go to hell once he died was now front and center in his mind. Was this the end? Did he even have a soul? He felt like a flame on a candlewick about to be extinguished.

———

Colette heard her brother's tormented cries through the walls around her. Jermain's muffled cries of agony more and more painful for her to hear. *Please, Jermain, fight back!*

Colette kicked her feet against the coffin and slammed her fists to the sides, attempting with all her strength to break through her confinement. Her hope faltered. She pressed her ear to the side of the coffin and heard Jermain's shouts and cries, foreign sounds. She'd never heard him scream and cry in such a terrible way, and it pained her to listen, unable to retaliate.

She had to find a way out. She had to help her brother, or they would all die.

———

Jermain thrashed and flailed his head, knocking the metallic file from Alexandru's clutch. Through a mouthful of blood, he asked, "Why?" He was barely able to get the words out. "Why are you doing this?"

"Little lamb, embrace your slaughter quietly, gracefully," Alexandru hissed, no longer resembling the vampire who'd entered their dwelling. He now looked more like Şerban had—a thousand-year-old relic from the underworld. He grasped Jermain's neck once again, squeezing hard with his cadaverous fingers. "You're not fit to be a part of our tribe." Alexandru dug his fangs into Jermain's neck and began to greedily guzzle the young vampire's blood.

"Please—" Jermain protested through a swollen mouthful of blood. "Stop. Please."

"Şerban—" Alexandru said, as he lifted his head from Jermain's neck, blood dripping from his mouth and down his decayed chin. "Was my brother." His fist smashed Jermain's head.

Jermain's vision turned black. His consciousness flashed on and off like a lighthouse beam.

In an instant, Alexandru was knocked forward into Jermain, his hold loosening. Jermain looked down and saw a steel spike piercing the front of Alexandru's coat. The old vampire clutched at the metal spike, his blood shooting out through the pipe like a spigot.

Jermain, through a sliver opening of his swollen left eye,

caught a glimpse of his father choking Alexandru from behind with something wrapped around Alexandru's neck. A wire?

Alexandru writhed about, struggling against whatever held him. Seeing his opportunity, Jermain pounced on Alexandru. Now, the three vampires wrestled, the conflict violent with growls and cries. With Charles on his back, Alexandru sprang to the ceiling, smashing into the bare lightbulb. After a few more minutes of struggle, Jermain heard clicking on the stairs. The echo of the door opening, slamming shut trailed down the cellar.

Jermain found matches in his jacket pocket and lit a candle. He surveyed the cellar and saw his father crouched on one knee, his face pale, holding his shoulder with an agonized look. Jermain panned the candle around the room, searching for Colette, but did not see her. And the old vampire had disappeared.

Too badly injured and weary to chase after him, Jermain went to his father, carefully examining his bloodied shoulder as his father groaned in pain. He helped Charles to his feet and they stood there for a moment, steadying each other while they looked around.

At the base of the stairs, Jermain noticed something shiny. "Do you see that?" Jermain asked, pointing toward the floor.

Charles limped over to it and picked it up. In the dim candle light, Jermain saw Colette's necklace shining in his father's grasp, the clasp broken.

"Where's Colette?" Jermain asked, his heart clenching. "Where is my sister?"

PART TWO

INTERLUDE

CHAPTER 1

1462

IT WAS EARLY MORNING, June 19th 1462, when Meleki rode into the Hoia Baciu forest on his Turkmen horse. Meleki, a janissary who had not taken part in the battle against Vlad and his army, was grateful to be alive, since they'd heard the prior night from their generals the Ottoman army had lost. He was in Bucharest on a different assignment, eighty kilometers southeast from where the battle took place. He'd been fortunate his post earlier that week had been switched at the last minute to guard the Danube River crossing at Giurgiu, instead of being sent to die at Târgoviște.

He rode alongside fourteen other janissaries—high-ranking officials and leaders in the Ottoman army. All Meleki thought about was how, through sheer luck, he would return home to see his family again. The generals weren't sure yet how many casualties there'd been, but they speculated several thousand dead. Their duty now—Meleki's mandate—was to take account of the battle's aftermath and attempt to rescue any man who may have survived Vlad Dracula's onslaught.

Meleki and his horse trudged deeper into the forest through thick gray fog that blanketed the riders as they raced along. The sky was dull and overcast, and it was unusually cold for a mid-June morning. The horse's hooves thudded in rhythm as they crushed twigs and leaves with their passage. The smell of gunpowder from the cannons two days earlier still lingered in the air—a sulfur veil that invaded Meleki and his men's nostrils. Târgoviște, he was informed, became a hellscape the day of the battle.

It was odd, Meleki thought, they hadn't stumbled upon any casualties from the battle yet. *There should be thousands of fallen soldiers*, Meleki thought. Where were they?

The horses hurtled past polearms, daggers, axes, maces and bows dropped during the fight, yet no fallen soldiers could be seen anywhere. Hundreds of arrows were drilled into the trees they passed.

They rode for another half kilometer until Meleki and the other men's horses ground to an abrupt halt, as soon as they'd come to a clearing in the forest. A few of the horses began to weave from side to side and snorted, appearing frustrated at what lay before them. The men were silent, for the site of what they'd stumbled upon made their hearts quiver with fear.

Stakes, varying from six to nine feet in length, buttressed a sea of Ottoman soldiers high into the heavens. The stakes were driven through the victim's body's—in through their lower regions, their rectums, and either out through their chests, backs, some even protruding from their mouths and necks. One of the commanding officers on horseback became sick at the sight. In the distance they heard painful groans and muffled voices. Many of the impaled soldiers, it appeared, were still alive.

The Ottomans were no strangers to impalement.

Impalement, as a method of torture, had been used by rulers and armies across many lands for over a thousand years. The terror Meleki felt, as the horses trudged closer to the site, came from the sheer number of impalement victims. The sounds of the dying and of the howling from all directions heightened Meleki's heartrate. He could almost feel the other janissaries' alarm as the horses they rode moved closer together, urged by their riders. Men who thought they'd seen it all, Meleki thought, began to look light-headed with fear in their eyes. Voices of the impaled writhing in pain, somehow still conscious, made Meleki think that perhaps he'd been killed in battle and his soul had ended up in hell.

As they entered into the nucleus of the dead, they saw there were not just men and soldiers who had been impaled, but women and children as well. One woman was spiked with her baby in tow.

Meleki turned to the other riders and yelled, "Look for any person still alive and, if they are still breathing, immediately put them out of their misery."

"Yes, sir," one of the men responded in their native Ottoman tongue. The janissaries, now given purpose, rode into the clearing, searching for anyone they might give mercy to.

Vlad did not play by any rules nor any military law of arms established by Sultan Mehmed II, the Sultan of the Ottoman Empire. He spat on whatever rules of war existed; a nonconformist when it came to the art of killing and murdering. He was an artist in pain, suffering, and death, and the forest Meleki rode through was Vlad's canvas.

Moving past a sea of death, Meleki figured there were thousands of victims, most already dead, having bled to death within an hour of their impaling. Many unfortunate souls, somehow, remained alive. For Vlad Dracula, an impalement of a victim who remained alive for a drawn-out length of time was a success.

Meleki heard groans, agonizing cries, and wails, but it was difficult to pinpoint where they came from. There were too many victims, most already dead. Something in the distance caught Meleki's attention. There appeared to be a small group of people on the ground rambling near a cluster of stakes. He reached for his dagger, unsure whether they were soldiers from Vlad's army who remained behind.

"Forward," Meleki instructed his horse. He maneuvered the horse towards the figures.

As Meleki approached, he saw three women gathered around a staked victim. They wore long black dresses, black embroidered blouses, and all three wore dark headscarves. Elaborate necklaces and earrings dangled from their necks and ears. Meleki heard them chanting something in the distance, but he was still too far to make out what they were saying.

Once Meleki was close enough, still on his horse, he addressed the trio. "Who are you? What are you doing here?" He squinted hard, scrutinizing them.

One of the women held a bowl to collect drops of blood from the impalement victim—a male soldier. Meleki appraised the soldier, but couldn't tell if he was dead or alive. The women continued praying and chanting, ignoring Meleki's presence.

Meleki did not recognize the language or the words they spoke.

"I am with the Ottoman army and you must answer me now." Meleki raised his voice. "Who are you? What are you doing here?" He knew they could hear him. He dismounted with his dagger in hand and, scowling, approached the women. Why were they not doing as he asked?

"Ladies," Meleki addressed the women. "Answer me when I address you." He marched towards them, his right hand gripping his dagger.

"You shall answer me," Meleki yelled, his patience gone.

One of the women swiveled her head towards Meleki. Meleki gasped at the sight of her. Her face was lined with cracks, wrinkles, and deep ridges. What alarmed Meleki the most was her eyes. She had no pupils. They were all black, like two obsidian stones, staring at him with a vacant look. Her lips were still moving, chanting unintelligible words.

A loud cracking sound drew Meleki's attention to his right. One of the stakes had snapped in the middle and was falling directly towards him. A man, along with the stake he was impaled on, collapsed. Meleki dove out of the way just before the body and stake fell on him. It crashed to the ground with a heavy impact, missing him by inches.

Meleki sprang back to his feet and looked toward where the three women had been standing.

They were gone.

CHAPTER 2

SAINT CASIMIR

DAYS HAD TURNED to weeks and weeks turned to months as Prince Casimir Jagiellon lay in bed, his cough worsening. The white death struck the prince of Poland at a young age. He was only twenty-five when he fell ill.

His younger brother, Sigismund I, held his hand while he lay in bed. Casimir remained optimistic as he lay ill, hoping his affliction would pass and he would become well again.

"How bad is the pain today?" Sigismund asked.

"I would prefer to speak about other topics, Sigi—politics, ethics, philosophy, religion— it will take my mind off the pain." Casimir coughed. He continued, his voice low and hoarse: "There is light and dark in the world. The blood we've shed during our military campaigns was not without result. We must continue to shine our light to the world."

Sigismund said nothing, just held his brother's hand. He'd offered to bring him more opium, but the young prince declined.

"God will judge me for my sins, but I know, in my soul, through my penance and my faith in the Lord, I will be granted entry into heaven. That is all you need, Sigi. Don't ever lose faith in the Lord and you will be saved." Casimir struggled to get the words out.

A deep, racking cough shook him. He hacked phlegm into his handkerchief. There was blood all over it. His brother took the handkerchief from him, folded it to a clean side, and wiped his mouth clean.

"Don't exert yourself, brother," Sigismund said. "You must reserve your strength."

After another coughing fit subsided, Casimir continued: "There are great lands beyond what the mapmakers have drawn thus far. The Portuguese—" He coughed again, but continued. "—are pushing the limits and discovering treasures beyond anything any of us have ever seen before." His voice was strained, but he pushed on. "More importantly, there are people there, non-believers, who can be turned into followers. Our mission should be to convert these infidels."

Casimir clutched his gold rosary and held it up. It glimmered in the sun's rays that streaked through the tall chamber windows. "The Church's mission—the same mission the Spanish and the Portuguese Kings have taken upon themselves—to convert the Pagans and non-believers. That should be our mission as well." He waved his gold rosary in the air, like heralding a sacred artifact, with the little strength he had. "Our aim should not be to simply plunder lands. We must not forget that, if we have no followers, this is all for nought. We cannot take these riches with us when we arrive at the Heavenly gates."

When Sigismund reached out to help him, Casimir clasped his brother's hands. "Promise me you will carry the word of God, the word of Christ, and also continue to fight against evil long after I'm gone; long after I'm buried. Remind those that the light of God—that good shall always triumph over evil."

Casimir exhaled in a soft rush, weary after having spoken for such a long stretch of time.

His brother laid a hand on Casimir's sweaty brow. "Rest, brother. You need to avoid exertion in order to get better. Do you need me to bring you anything? Anything at all?"

"I am fine, Sigi," the prince said, his voice weak. "Pray with me."

They clasped hands, closed their eyes, and prayed the Lord's prayer.

PART THREE

THE BLACK MARKET

NYC – 2004

IT WAS eight-twenty in the evening, just after supper, when Principal Richard pressed the power key to his PC and booted up his computer. The fans came alive, whirring noisily, as did the lights on the front of the machine. It was a custom PC he'd rigged himself with the highest-rated parts and equipment that allowed him to trade stocks on a brokerage platform, bid on expensive art on high-end auction sites, and use Tor—the software application he used to browse the dark web.

He logged into Tor and typed *Hidden Wiki* into his browser, a site he visited when he wanted to scour the black market. Principal Richard clicked his mouse and scrolled down the page. A mix of gothic and industrial fonts on a black background read: *guns, drugs, sex (escorts), weapons.* He scrolled down and down a lengthy list of nefarious links and clicked on *hitman.* A new webpage opened with a title that read: *Murder for hire.* Scrolling further, Richard clicked on another link that brough him to a page where he could *checkout* with a price that read: $15,000 *USD*.

Principal Richard uploaded a photograph of Rick De Luca and typed in the teenager's information. He plugged in Rick's name, age, birthday, address, school, then uploaded additional information requested. Clicking a few more times with his mouse, Richard fished a credit card from his desk, input the payment data and, in one last final stroke of his finger, he clicked *submit*.

"What's done is done," Principal Richard whispered to himself.

———

Later that evening, Jermain sat in front of his desktop computer and opened his email, and clicked on the new inquiry he'd received with information pertaining to:

Rick De Luca

Jermain shot up from his chair and barged into Colette's bedroom. She lounged comfortably on her futon reading a magazine when he charged in. "Colette, we got an inquiry!" Jermain tried to keep his excitement under control, waiting to see how his sister reacted.

"Murder?" Colette asked, her eyes still glued to the magazine.

"Yeah! It's for a kid that goes to Saint Thomas Prep."

Colette closed the magazine and shifted her eyes until they met her brother's. They gleamed with intense interest.

"It's not for Cas, right?" she asked. Jermain noted there was a glint of fear in her eyes.

He shook his head. "Nah, it's for another kid. Rick. Rick De Luca."

Colette looked relieved. "Don't think I know him," Colette said, returning her attention to the magazine.

Jermain stood in her room, saying nothing for a moment. She looked back up at him and made a face. Jermain smiled. He loved busting her chops.

"What, do you have the hots for Cas now or something?"

"Yeah, I am so hot for Casimir. I can't wait to drink his saintly blood," she said with a scoffing tone, turning her gaze back to what she was reading.

"We need his blood for Father," Jermain said sternly. "We're not going to drink his blood."

"Just a taste? A drop?" she begged, flashing fangs.

"Okay, maybe just a little taste." Jermain relaxed, with a small curling smile. Smiles were a rare occurrence on Jermain's face. After all they'd been through, to find blood from a saint—in this case the descendant of a saint—after all these years, Jermain was curious to find out what such special blood would taste like.

CHAPTER 2
JOEY'S PIZZERIA

SITTING on the hood of his Honda Civic, Cas passed the joint to Seth. Jazzie bopped her head and sang along to *All My Loving* by The Beatles playing from the Honda's stereo. They had the radio dialed in on the oldies station. Paul McCartney's vocals flooded the open-air roof parking garage of a small shopping center—the hangout they'd drive to on clear summer nights. Most stores at the shopping plaza—*Sam Goody, Barnes & Noble, The Gap*—would be closing down soon. The security guard would let them hang out there until eleven-thirty or midnight, and there weren't many other people or cars around. It was Cas' sanctuary from school and work, and he knew it was solace for the siblings. Hanging out in the parking garage for Jazzie and Seth was a much-needed break from caring for their father who, Cas was told, was dying and didn't have much time to live.

"I saw them, you know," Jazzie said, then blew a stream of smoke from the joint. "They were incredible. The best rock band I've ever seen."

"Saw who?" Cas asked.

"The Beatles," Jazzie said, then continued to sing along for a moment before adding, "At City Park Stadium in New Orleans."

Cas guffawed at her comment.

"That's not possible. They haven't played a show in over..." It took Cas a moment. "...thirty years. And we're..."

"Seventeen years old," Seth chimed in, then took a heavy toke from the joint.

"So you're full of shit." Cas laughed. *Why does she lie so much?* Cas thought.

This wasn't the first time she'd claimed she'd witnessed or experienced something from long before she was born. He figured she was a compulsive liar, and maybe she needed to see a therapist. He put up with her lying, though. *Is this what love is? Am I in love?* She could've told him she'd met Jesus Christ and he'd have gone along with her story, nodding in agreement all along the way. Tonight, he'd decided to stray from just going along with her and called her out on her BS. They were still only friends, but he sensed there might be something more than platonic simmering. He was just waiting for the right opportunity to make his move.

"Yeah, you're right, Cas." She lowered her head. "I'm full of shit. There's no way I could've been there because they played...they were around before I was born," Jazzie said. It almost looked like a tear was forming in her eye, but there was something unusual about it. The tear looked red under the blue-tone light of the tall parking lot lights.

Cas pivoted, lightening the mood, after noticing her apparent sadness.

"My mom told me about the day Lennon was shot," he said with a smile. "She remembers it like it was yesterday. She's a big Beatles fan too, you know."

"Yeah? Your mom is so sweet." Jazzie's spirits seemed to lift, just for a second.

Seth took another hit from the joint, then passed it to Cas. "I'm heading home. I haven't eaten anything all day," he said, plopping off the hood of the Civic.

"Do you want me to give you a ride?" Cas asked.

"Nah, it's all right. I'm in the mood for a walk." Seth straightened the hem of his T-shirt. "I have a lot on my mind. I can use some alone time."

"Everything okay?" Cas asked.

Seth nodded. "Yeah, everything's cool, man. Can you give Jazzie a ride home later?"

"Of course. I'll drop her off."

Cas didn't mind being the designated driver. He didn't drink much. And he was an okay driver despite being high on marijuana.

Cas observed Jazzie and wondered what she might be thinking about. He gazed at her red hair intertwined with her fine grays. *Fascinating.* He felt like he'd been stuck in this awkward in-between stage with her. He sensed she liked him, too, but he didn't know how to make that leap to break out of the dreaded friendzone. There was a barrier he needed to pierce through, but he was at a loss as to how he'd penetrate it.

Seth left, leaving Jazzie and Cas alone, sitting close to each other atop the hood of the Civic. Cas couldn't think of anything to spark up a conversation. He looked over at her, opened his mouth to say something, but only stared. She gazed up into the inky canvas that was infinite space. The night was clouded with atmospheric haze and light pollution, limiting their ability to see many stars. If you strained your eyes, there were a couple of bright specks poking through the city's shrouded night sky.

"See that bright, yellowish-white light there?" Jazzie pointed her index finger in the direction of a bright light in her field of vision.

"Where?" Cas squinted, struggling to see where she was pointing.

"There."

Jazzie took Cas' finger and pointed it in the direction of the light until he locked in on it.

"Right... there!"

"I see it now." Cas smiled, relishing her chilly touch.

"That's Saturn."

"Really?" Cas was amazed at how intelligent Jazzie was. She was an encyclopedia of knowledge. She knew so much about history and the world it made him feel inferior in her presence.

"That's so cool," he said. Realizing the joint was nearly done, Cas carefully stubbed what was left, extinguishing it. He took out a small Ziploc bag from his pants pocket and he slid it in, saving it for another time.

"Somewhere up there, Ra is sailing through the night on the Mesektet," Jazzie said. "Fighting off Apophis."

"What?" Cas asked, his eyes dilated. Sometimes she didn't make sense, at least not in the state he was in.

"Nothing."

Jazzie's gaze hadn't shifted from the night sky and the stars.

"How come I never see you eat?" Cas asked.

Jazzie froze for a second, looking surprised. Her expression turned scornful. It looked as if she were thinking, *why did you go there?*

Why did I go there? he thought to himself. He felt a pang of hunger, realizing he hadn't eaten anything since lunch time and it was now very late. He'd thought back to all of the times he'd hung out with Jazzie and her brother, and he'd never seen them eat. Ever. He'd eaten in their company, but they always drummed up some excuse to not join him. They'd claim they'd eaten already or they couldn't have such and such food because it didn't agree with their stomachs. Yada, yada, yada. Always the same excuse. He figured they still had time to grab a slice of pizza. Joey's Pizzeria was open and they could still make it there before it closed.

The stalled tear Cas had seen earlier made its way down Jazzie's soft, white cheek. Her tear, a red drop of cherry juice, glissaded down her pale cheek. Cas reached out to touch her cheek with the back of his hand, and then studied the moisture.

"You're bleeding." Cas couldn't keep the worry from his voice.

"Oh, no. Am I?" Jazzie covered her face with her hands.

Cas tried to pull her hands away to take a look at her, but she pushed him away.

"Please, Cas. I want to be left alone."

He stopped trying to move her hands, but asked, "Are you hurt?"

"No," she sniffled. "I'm just sad."

"What are you so sad about?"

There was a long moment of silence before Jazzie answered, "Everything."

Cas reached for her again, but stopped himself. "Do you want to talk about it?"

Jazzie lowered her hands and shook her head. "No. Not right now. Can you take me home, please?"

"Yeah, sure."

. . .

The silence during the car ride back to Jazzie's was oppressive. Cas tried to drum up something to say, something to spark up conversation, but his mind was full of nothing but questions he couldn't ask. He wondered why what he'd said had upset her so much. It was a valid question in his mind. *Did she have an eating disorder?* He didn't think so. She looked well-nourished, for the most part. Apart from her skin always feeling cold and her complexion appearing wan from time to time (anemia?), she didn't appear to be malnourished.

Now, he was second-guessing himself. *Did they have enough money to eat? Were they poor?* Cas knew they spent a lot of their time and resources caring for their father, whom he hadn't met, or even seen, yet. But Jazzie was very active and athletic. The two of them had gone on night bike rides for miles and miles all over the city. It amazed him how she would never tire. Odd he'd never really seen her drink any water either. *She definitely has an issue with food,* he thought. *Better to leave that topic alone. Especially if I'm ever going to have a chance to get to know her better.*

The car rolled to a stop in front of Jazzie's house. Cas turned, wanting to give her a friendly kiss on the cheek but, before he could make his move, she'd opened the door and bolted from the car.

"Thank you for the ride, Cas. I'll talk to you later." Her words drifted back to him as she made her way to her front door.

"Bye, Jazzie." Cas wasn't sure she'd even heard him as she dashed inside her house.

He ached to kiss her—not some innocent peck on the cheek, that was for grandmas—but a *real* kiss. The thought of his own pathetic cowardice, of all the chances he'd let slip by, made his stomach turn, and he decided right then and there he was done being afraid.

Cas stared at the stale pizza behind the glass counter at Joey's Pizzeria. It was half-past midnight and there was a young couple eating at a table but, besides them and the baker, the pizzeria was desolate.

Still stoned, he muttered, "Can I just have one slice, please?"

"Just one?" the Hispanic man behind the counter asked, his tone brusque.

"Yeah, thanks."

The man scooped up the slice with a thin metal peel and tossed it into the oven. Cas turned his attention to a small CRT television near the ceiling in a corner of the pizzeria. A breaking news report on the fuzzy screen caught his attention. The female reporter stood in front of yellow *Do Not Cross* tape.

"We are live in front of Grove Park in Queens, New York, where police found a murder scene."

Red and blue police lights flashed off the reporter's face as she spoke into the microphone. The dark oak trees and dense bushes crowding her backdrop sent a chill through Casimir's flesh.

"At approximately ten-forty five this evening, a seventeen-year-old male was found brutally murdered in the park. Pedestrians found his body and called police to the scene. No further details have been provided by the NYPD. We'll update you as more information becomes available."

A seventeen-year-old male, replayed in Cas' mind. The dark woods, looming ominously in the background, haunted his thoughts. The kid had been the same age as him. It wasn't a good idea to travel through those parks alone late at night, thought Cas, although it wasn't real late and Grove Park was a popular hangout. A few of his friends had thrown a kegger there just a few weeks before. His stomach churned as he watched the breaking news report. Something about the reporter standing in front of such a familiar setting stirred an unsettling feeling in his bones.

CHAPTER 3

TOO CLOSE TO HOME

THE FOLLOWING MONDAY, Cas sat in homeroom thinking about all the assignments he had due that day: the introductory paragraph for his AP social studies paper, two advanced calculus problems that had consumed almost two hours to solve, and the scenes he'd read for *Hamlet*. It was a mental checklist he worked over every morning while he allowed his brain to simmer before his teachers began battering him with rigorous academic nonsense (*all right, so some of it was useful and could be applied to the real world*) that made his brain tired.

Principal Richard's even voice cracked through the PA system, just as it usually did at eight fifteen every morning.

"Good morning to all students, staff, and all those present at Saint Thomas Academy on this beautiful seventh of June. I would like to begin with our tradition of reciting the angelic salutation: Hail, Mary, full of grace, the Lord is with thee. Blessed art thou amongst women and blessed is the fruit of thy womb, Jesus. Holy Mary, Mother of God, pray for us sinners, now and at the hour of our death. Amen."

The students and homeroom teacher, in unison, replied, "Amen." Next, the principal recited the Pledge of Allegiance. After the pledge followed the reporting of all the athletic events that had taken place over the weekend.

He continued, "Our lacrosse team managed to secure a win over Sanctuary Prep on Saturday, defeating them eleven to eight. Congratulations to James Halleran, who scored a staggering eight of our eleven goals."

A short spatter of applause ensued.

Lacrosse was a big deal at Saint Thomas for reasons Casimir would never care to understand. He was a BMXer, an extreme sports enthusiast, and never really pursued team sports after middle school.

"I have some sad news to report," he continued. "It is not a common occurrence that we lose one of our students. This past weekend, we suffered the unfortunate loss of Rick De Luca. Rick was just a few weeks away from graduating from Saint Thomas Preparatory and was on his way to attending Iona University. Those of you who knew Rick, most likely knew him as a caring, compassionate and dedicated student at Saint Thomas."

Cas snorted. *That's absolute bullshit. You hated him and wanted to kick him out of school for years but, instead, you took his father's money and let him coast.*

"Arrangements have been made at D'Angelo Funeral Home in Howard Beach for this Wednesday evening from four to seven p.m. and Thursday from four to eight p.m. I, along with the staff and administration at Saint Thomas, are truly sorry for the loss of our young scholar. May Rick rest in peace and experience mercy and happiness in heaven. If you were close with Rick and need to speak to someone about this matter, Mr. Zambrano's door is always open. You can find him in room three-thirteen. That is all

I have for you today. I wish you all a wonderful school day."

"What the hell happened to Rick?" Andrew asked, as he bit into his turkey sandwich, looking around the table.

The boys—Cas, Andrew, Mike, Stan, and Pete—sat together in the center of the cafeteria. They'd had the same table since freshman year, united by their mutual love of hardcore hip-hop, heavy metal and marijuana.

The cafeteria was quieter than usual, with only a soft murmur of voices instead of the usual chaos and loud chatter. A dark cloud hung somberly over the students as they ate their lunch.

Casimir took out his sandwich from a brown paper bag and peeled back the tin foil his mother had meticulously wrapped around it.

"They're not releasing much information. All people know so far is he was murdered by some psychopath," Stan said, before taking a drink of soda.

"Was he shot?" Cas asked.

"Don't think so. My dad says he was butchered. Might've been stabbed or something along those lines," Mike said in a matter-of-fact tone.

"How do you know he was stabbed?" Cas asked.

"I have my sources," Mike said with a smirk. "If I told you then I'd have to kill you."

Mike did have his sources. His father was a big-wig attorney with contacts throughout the New York City legal system and NYPD and might know more than the general public.

"Real morbid, man." Cas shook his head, not entertained by Mike's callousness. Sure, Rick De Luca wasn't the most well-liked student at Saint Thomas. If most students were completely honest, they'd classify him as a complete piece of crap. But the murder, Rick's murder, was too close to home. Cas hadn't known anyone his age who had died, let alone known anyone his age who had been murdered. The situation was made more unsettling because it had occurred in a park they all frequented often. It was sometimes used as a shortcut to cut through neighborhoods. And now, it seemed, there was a real-life Jack the Ripper in their backyard.

"Are you guys going to the wake?" Andrew asked, eyeing each of them in turn.

"I'm not. I didn't really talk to him," Stan said with a shrug.

"I think we should go," Cas said. "Even though I wasn't close with him, none of us were close with him, I feel like we should go pay our respects...a life was lost. And it could've been any one of us."

A grim curiosity took over his thoughts. One of his classmates had been brutally murdered and it frightened him to his core. *What if Rick had been targeted? What if his murder wasn't random?* Cas wasn't sure why such an absurd thought had crossed his mind, but Rick was the sort of person who could have had an enemy or two. It had been just over forty-eight hours and no one had yet been arrested for the crime. *It's very hard to commit a murder without getting caught.* Cas thought about the crime shows about New York he'd watched. *The NYPD were shrewd, had eyes everywhere and worked swiftly to solve crimes.*

"I'll go if you go," Andrew said.

Cas glanced over at the table where Rick used to sit. Casey and Samuel, two of Rick's only friends, were being consoled by a few female classmates who sat near their lunch table. Samuel's eyes were puffy and welled with tears. Cas had heard Sam had been with Rick just an hour before he was murdered. Rick had been on his way home from Sam's house, which explained why he'd been cutting through the park.

For Cas and his schoolmates, death had once been a foreign concept only thought about when one's grandparent or an elderly relative or neighbor passed away. It was still rare for a parent or sibling to die, though Cas did lose his father when he was only ten years old. But no one their age died. Now, it was a real, palpable notion that had snuck up on them unannounced. And their only recourse, they were told, was to say a prayer for their dead schoolmate. Cas felt life was one giant pinball machine. Sometimes you could hit the ball with the flippers and keep going; keep playing the game. But other times, almost randomly, it seemed, the ball slipped right through the center of those flippers, and it all ended: game over.

Andrew smoked a cigarette leaning against the wall near the entrance of the E train station, blowing gray puffs of smoke into the drab New York afternoon sky. He flicked his cigarette away, crushing it under his worn dress shoes as Cas approached.

Cas and Andrew sat one space apart from each other on a bench in the subway car as the train barreled through the tunnel. The subway was packed with commuters and students either heading to their night shifts or on their way back home after a long, arduous day at work or school.

"Are you coming over on Friday? I should be getting my Volcano this week," Andrew said.

"I'll let you know later this week. I might be hanging out with Seth and Jazzie."

Andrew looked away and frowned. "Are you and Jazzie an item yet?"

Cas felt his cheeks redden and shook his head. "No, not yet. I'm still waiting for the right moment to make a move. It's kind of weird that I'm good friends with her brother, too." Cas clutched his backpack. "You know?"

"You think he'd get pissed if you hook up with her?"

Cas frowned, because he'd wondered the same thing. "I'm not sure. I really like her, though. We have a lot in common. What's going on with you and Jackie?"

Andrew shrugged. "It's going all right. We're going to hang out on Saturday."

"What are you guys gonna do?"

"We're gonna go to the movies, then probably hang out at my place." Andrew leaned back and closed his eyes.

Cas poked him. "What movie are you gonna see?"

"*The Day After Tomorrow.*"

"I want to see that." Cas loved movies. They took him away from his own dull existence for a couple of hours, and he could pretend his life wasn't so boring.

Andrew sat up and smiled at him. "Bring Jazzie. We can make it a double date."

Cas didn't reply, thinking over and considering Andrew's proposal. "I guess I should."

"You have her number yet?"

Cas sighed. "No. She's really weird about giving out her phone number. She says her dad doesn't allow her to give her number to boys."

Andrew laughed. "Are you serious, dude? You think she's a virgin? Has she ever had a boyfriend? She's seventeen, isn't she?"

"I don't know. I haven't exactly asked her about her sex life. I have no idea if she's ever had a boyfriend. And I think she's sixteen, not seventeen"

Cas' face heated up as the subject matter became uncomfortable. He didn't enjoy talking about sex with anyone. All he could think about was how he was the last of his friends to lose his virginity. Andrew lost his two summers ago. Maybe he'd pop his cherry with Jazzie. The thought made him excited and nervous all at once. If they got drunk together at a party and the setting was just right, it could definitely happen.

"You said she's homeschooled, right?" Andrew asked.

"Yeah, her and her brother have private tutors. She's incredibly smart," Cas said, trying to keep his voice even.

Andrew made a face. "That's weird. Did she ever go to a school? Like an actual school building?"

"She did when she lived in New Orleans." Cas had wondered about that, too, but he'd been afraid to ask her. "It works out for her, though, because she does so much to take care of her father."

"What happened to her mother?"

"I'm not sure. Her mom's not in the picture. She never mentions her and I don't want to pry," Cas said. "Not sure if she died or her parents got divorced but it seems like her mom's been out of the picture for a while now. It's probably a sensitive subject if she's never brought it up and I'm not gonna dare ask her about it."

THERE WAS a long line of mourners formed outside of D'Angelo Funeral Home when Cas and Andrew arrived. They met Mike and Pete outside and started towards the entrance where friends and family members congregated, waiting their turn in line to pay their respects.

Casimir didn't recognize most people present since he hadn't been friends with Rick De Luca.

The crowd of solemn faced lamentadores entered through the double doors of the funeral home. Women cried into tissues while most young children remained stoic, too young to truly understand the ramifications and finality of death.

The line Casimir and his friends stood on plodded along slowly, drawing closer to the casket. Cas looked up and saw Rick's parents, and two young girls (his sisters?), who stood next to the copper casket. The color of their faces had been completely drained by grief. While Mr. De Luca stood firm, more composed, his wife's face twisted in anguish as she wept, clutching at the tissues in her hands.

"How did you know Rick?" Mrs. De Luca asked Cas as

he stood directly in front of her, tears pouring down her face.

"I go to Saint Thomas. I was his classmate. I'm so sorry for your loss, Mrs. De Luca." Cas gave Mrs. De Luca a quick handshake, then shook Mr. De Luca's hand. "My sincerest condolences to you and your family."

Mr. De Luca wasn't crying, but Cas could tell he had been, his eyes red and lined with bags, most likely from not having slept all week.

Cas stepped over, stood in front of the casket and glanced down at Rick, whose eyes were closed. *Of course, they were closed. What'd you expect, dummy?* His classmate lay dressed in a designer suit, his hair combed and styled back with gel, and his face caked with mortuary makeup.

Cas' eyes gravitated to Rick's neck where, through the thick makeup, he could see two rosy spots. The spots, covered with concealer and foundation, didn't fool anyone. The sight of these spots made Cas' skin goose up. *Maybe that happened during the attack,* Cas thought. *What kind of weapon could make marks even makeup couldn't cover?*

A weathered-looking waitress holding a notepad and pencil and smelling like cigarettes and bacon, asked the boys for their orders. She chewed gum the way a horse chews cud, and her voice was low and gruff.

"Let me get..." Andrew skimmed the menu. "...a Philly Cheesesteak, please."

"Would you like fries or a salad?"

"Fries, please." Andrew handed over his menu and she tucked it under her notepad.

"And you?" Her eyes were on Cas.

"I'll have a cheeseburger with fries, please."

Eyes down, she prodded, "How would you like it cooked?"

"Medium rare, please."

The diner was alive with the night crowd. The boys, Cas, Andrew, Mike and Pete, sat in a booth, their ties loosened and their moods quiet—numb and dejected. Though none of the boys had been close with Rick, the reality of his death, the crying, the grieving of his family and friends, had a palpable effect on them.

"Did anyone notice those marks on his neck?" Cas asked.

"I saw them," Pete said, his voice quiet. "What the fuck was that?"

"The mortician tried to cover them up with makeup, but no amount of makeup could hide that crap." Mike lowered his head, looking at the scratched table top.

The waitress dropped off their sodas, and went away again.

"I don't know, but it looked like he got poked there or something," Cas mused.

"It looked like he got stabbed with brazing forks," Pete added, nodding. "Was that how he was killed? Stabbed right in the neck?" Pete grimaced.

"I can't believe they haven't caught the killer yet," Andrew grumbled. He looked around as if expecting someone to contradict him. "He looked really skinny. Was he always that skinny?"

"There might be more murders like this," Mike said.

"What do you mean?" Cas asked.

"They've found some other bodies around New York City with similar marks on their necks. I read an article in the paper a few weeks ago that described murder victims having similar wounds." Andrew hunched over the table, lowering his voice. "One article described them as bite marks."

"What the fuck?" Pete's eyes were wide. "Vampires?"

"There're some sick fucking people out there." Mike sat up in his chair, his eyes darting around the room.

"They've found three victims with similar wounds on their necks so far this year." The boys, all slack-jawed, focused on Mike as he imparted what seemed like top-secret information. He knew something they didn't. And it wasn't just because his father worked in the legal system. Mike followed the news and stayed informed. He read a lot. He knew what went on in and around the entire city.

Mike continued, "Rick is the fourth victim who's been found with puncture wounds on his neck. This doesn't seem like a coincidence. There may be an active serial killer out there." He took a long drink of his soda before continuing. "I brought it up with my dad and he didn't confirm or deny it but, from what he told me, the police are on the lookout for whoever's killing people with a pair of sharp spikes."

"Or fangs," Pete said. "Maybe we should get a hold of some stakes...and garlic." He grabbed hold of his cross. "I already have my cross."

"A serial killer." Cas stifled a groan. He felt his heart contract, tightening in his chest and making it hard for him to breathe. This was the sort of stuff one would only hear about on *Cold Case Files* or in movies. Horror movies. Now, it was a real thing in their backyard, happening right in their neighborhood. And someone they knew had been a serial killer's victim.

CHAPTER 5

CASIMIR

CAS LAY IN BED, his eyes closed, but his mind active. His head pounded. He'd stayed up late with his friends drinking beer the night before. Rick's wake had made them all think about their mortality—made them think that, perhaps, they weren't going to live forever. The melancholy they'd felt from seeing Rick's parents, his family, friends, and school-mates crying at the foot of his casket propelled them to buy forty-ounce bottles of beer and drink.

Cas' mom knocked on his door, the sound echoing through his aching head.

"Are you up yet?" She kept knocking.

Cas let out a loud groan.

"It's nearly eleven o'clock, Casimir. Get out of bed and come have some breakfast," she said from the other side of the door. She jiggled the door knob, attempting to open it, but Cas had locked it. "You can't sleep the day away," his mom said reprovingly.

Casimir grumbled, then turned in bed, hoping his mother would go away and leave him to his thoughts.

"I made pancakes." The knocking stopped.

Casimir rolled out of bed with a heavy sigh and made his way over to the door, opening it. He wiped away his eye gunk and saw the scowl on his mother's face. It always made him feel disappointed and it didn't sit well with him when his mother expressed disappointment with him.

"Want to go to church with me?" she asked with a faint smile. "I already ate, but I'll wait for you to get ready if you want to come along."

"I don't feel like going to church today."

Patricia sighed. "You always used to come to church with me. Now, you never want to go."

Cas shrugged. "I'm not a little kid anymore, ma. And church is boring. I hate the priest at St. Anthony's. Mass there is torture."

"Come on, then." His mother turned away and headed to the kitchen. "Breakfast."

They sat in silence at their small dining room table. Patricia read the newspaper with a concentrated look while Cas worked on his pancakes. He poured a generous amount of maple syrup on his breakfast. Patricia's hair was done up and she wore a nice dress, ready for twelve-thirty Sunday mass. She poured herself more coffee from the pot and broke the silence. "They haven't caught the person who killed Rick," she said.

"I know."

"I've been following this and a few other murders, and there's been talk that they could be related. There could be a serial killer on the loose. They're calling them the *Vampire Murders*." Patricia turned the newspaper article toward Cas. "Because of the marks they find on the victims' necks."

Cas didn't respond, and didn't look at the paper. He

focused on wolfing down his pancakes. His mind took him back to the two red marks on Rick's neck the night before. *Vampire Murders.* He tried to shrug off the association he'd formed. *What an eerie and outlandish epithet.*

"I don't want you staying out late at night." Patricia folded the paper, but he could feel her gaze on him. "Rick was murdered in Grove Park. I know you and your friends like to hang out there sometimes." He made the mistake of looking up at her. There was a worried look in her eyes. "Can you please just do me a favor and be careful when you go out." She leaned in and put her hand on his arm, her expression pleading.

"I'll be careful," Casimir said, trying to keep the irritation out of his voice. "Jesus, I'm not a little kid anymore. I'm going to college in a few months. What are you going to do when I leave?"

"I know you're not a little kid anymore. But you're still my child and I don't want anything to happen to you." His mother let out a sharp breath. "What I'm going to do when you're gone is miss you dearly, baby." She squeezed his cheek.

"Ow!" He shook away from her grasp and laughed. "Are you going to call me every day?" he asked.

"You better call me every day, mister! Just because you go away to college doesn't mean you stop loving and caring for your mother."

They both laughed.

———

The ultra-black walls of Colette's room were a perfect backdrop for the posters of her favorite bands. The Beatles, The Doors, The Ramones, Marilyn Manson, and others. A thick layer of film was slapped over the window, a necessary barrier against the hateful sun. Humans and their precious daylight, she thought. The small, stainless-steel coffin in the corner was a real conversation starter; she often wondered what story she'd invent if she ever let a human inside. She'd decorated the room with simple touches, a pathetic effort to make it feel like a young teenage girl's room, a desperate attempt to pretend she was still that bright-eyed girl from New Orleans with the whole world in front of her, and not a vampiress who'd been walking the earth for over one hundred years. It was a teenager's room, though, one no one would ever truly visit unless they were to be drained of their blood.

Colette hung upside down from a pull-up bar she'd bolted to her ceiling, her long hair brushing the floor. The inversion took some of the fire out of her back, a dull ache that still bothered her from the time she was shot by police in 1919. Those goddamn silver-plated bullets had done their damage, and her back was never quite the same after the incident on Ursulines Avenue. The searing pain of the silver tearing through her was a constant thrum of discomfort beneath her skin.

She reached for her cellphone and dialed.

"Hello?" Casimir answered on the other end.

She smiled. "Hey, Cas."

"Uh, who is this?"

"You seriously don't recognize my voice?" She thought about being offended, then shrugged it off. "Take a wild guess."

"Jazzie?"

"Duh. You really didn't recognize my voice?" She laughed.

He sounded pleased to hear from her. "What's up? I thought you didn't have a phone?"

"Who doesn't have a phone? Don't be silly." Colette paused. Then, "Listen, I have a big favor to ask you. Can you meet me later tonight?"

"Tonight? Uh, sure. Yeah. What do you need?"

"I'll discuss it when I see you." She wanted him to wonder. It meant he would think about her until their meeting.

"Okay," he said. "Where do you want to meet?"

"Meet me at Hillside Cemetery at ten."

"Ten? On a school night?"

There was a moment of silence.

"Fine, don't meet me, then." She let out a heavy sigh.

Cas sighed, but didn't say anything.

She thought for a moment. "Can you do nine?"

"Sure," came the quick reply. "Nine works. I just can't be out too late tonight. I have a presentation tomorrow in—"

Not allowing him to finish, she interrupted, "Sounds great, Cas. I'll see you near the fence where we can get in."

"Okay, see you tonight. Bye."

"Bye." Colette giggled then hung up.

She dropped her arms and continued to hang upside down for a while, thinking about whether she would be able to coax Casimir into agreeing to do her bidding.

———

Later that evening, Casimir stood in front of the fence of Hillside Cemetery where he and his friends used to sneak in through a hole in the wrought iron perimeter surrounding it. Cas stared down at the fence and sighed. He thought, for a moment, he was at the wrong location, but no, he'd arrived at the deserted area where he and his friends had once wandered amongst the tombstones after hours. The hole they'd used had been repaired, wired shut, and there was no way they were going to be able to get inside. The barbed wire that lined the top of the fence would cut them to ribbons if they attempted to climb over.

He glanced at his cell phone. Nine-o-seven. He crossed his arms. *Where is she?* he thought. *I can't be up late tonight. I have to do well on my final presentation tomorrow for AP history.*

Cas paced back and forth in front of the padlocked gate, trying to decide what Jazzie wanted here, of all places. He looked down at his phone again. *Should I call her? What if her brother or father picks up?*

He wondered what she had to talk to him about. Maybe she was going to profess her love for him once and for all. Fat chance. She must need a favor from him. But what on earth could it be?

Cas plopped down on the cement curb. A few minutes later, he heard light footfalls approach. He looked up and saw Jazzie, her red and gray curly hair bouncing, as she ran toward him.

"I'm so sorry I'm late," Jazzie said, sounding a bit out of breath as she arrived.

"Is everything okay?"

Jazzie's eyes were dilated. She took a moment to regain her breath before speaking again.

"Yeah, I'm really sorry. My dad wasn't feeling well."

Cas immediately asked, "Is he all right? What happened?"

"He's better now. He just had an—" Her eyes panned over the fence and narrowed when she noticed the fence had been wired shut. "...episode."

He followed her gaze to the fence. "How are we going to get in? Do you want to just walk along the sidewalk? What did you want to talk to me about?"

Jazzie reached in her back jean pocket and pulled out a pair of heavy-duty wire cutters. Approaching the fence, she began clipping the repaired patch with the wire cutters, creating a new opening for them to enter.

A wide grin formed on Cas' mouth. "You've got to be kidding me."

They strolled along the pathway, ambling past timeworn graves, mossy tombs and dark mausoleums, walking over cracks and fissures in the ancient stone path. It was an old cemetery, opened in 1848. The only illumination on their walk, save from the moon's distant gleam, came from the dim glow of far-off streetlights filtering through the iron gates.

"So what did you want to talk to me about?" Cas asked, his hands stuffed in his pockets.

"Do you believe in God?"

"I'm not..." He glanced over at her curiously. "I'm not sure if I do. Is that what you dragged me out here to talk about on a Sunday night? I have a big presentation tomorrow." Cas knew he sounded annoyed and immediately regretted his tone.

Although irritated he'd be up later than he would've wanted, Cas was captivated by the depth of Jazzie's thoughts. In the end, any time spent with Jazzie was time worth burning.

"What about—" Jazzie kept pace alongside him "—evil?"

"What about it?"

She glanced over at him, her expression uncertain. "Do you believe in evil? Like good and evil? Is it real or is it made up? I've been thinking about it for a long time. When people commit evil, is it real evil or is it—" She forced a smile. "—something made up to scare people into behaving?"

He thought about it for a moment, looking around him. "It's probably something made up to scare people, as far as religion goes, but there are evil people in the world. Don't you think so?" Cas asked. He looked over at her, but she was looking away toward some of the old graves, lost in her thoughts. A moment later, she tilted her head down and he thought she might've been counting the stones along the path or the number of graves.

"What was your father like?" she asked him.

"He was..." Cas was caught off guard. He hadn't anticipated *that* question. "Hard-headed," he continued. "Him and my mom always used to bicker. I remember that much." He laughed. "My mom would threaten to divorce him, but she never did. They loved each other. It was the real thing."

Cas stopped. "What's really on your mind," he asked. "What did you drag me out here to talk to me about?" Silence settled around them, and the hairs on the back of his neck stirred, as if they were surrounded by ghosts.

"I need to ask you for a favor, but you have to promise me..." Jazzie smiled, but didn't look him in the eyes. "...you won't tell anyone about this."

"Of course." He straightened. "If you need me to keep a secret, I won't tell a soul."

Jazzie paused for a long second, before taking a breath. "Okay. I need your help with something. Our father's really sick and we need to get him medicine. But the medicine's very expensive and his insurance won't cover it." She sighed, brushing her hair away from her face. "I thought of a way to make some quick money. A way we can all make some quick money."

"Who's we?" He frowned and shot her a quick glance.

There was a longer pause before she answered, turning to resume their walk as she went on. "You, Seth, and I."

"Yeah?" He should have expected that, but had hoped it could just be the two of them. He moved with her as they continued walking, wondering why Seth made him feel so uneasy. "Okay. What's your plan?"

"I've started selling drugs. It's actually a new—"

Cas interrupted. "Jazz, I'm sorry, but this sounds like something I don't want to be involved with."

"Just hear me out." Her eyes reddened.

Cas had never seen her act this desperate. She was practically begging him to help her out.

She continued: "It's a new type of drug. I was hoping you could help me sell it. You could make some money, too. I just need some help with this."

"Jesus."

"Could you help me out?" She looked up at him, but kept moving. They walked past gravestones dating back to the mid and late eighteen hundreds. Many graves were weather-beaten and eroded. Some epitaphs were no longer legible. "It would just be for a little while until we make enough money to pay for his medicine." She laid a slender hand on his arm. "We'll supply you with it. You just help us distribute it and you'll make a fair cut, too. It'll be worth it."

Cas gripped his hands together. "I don't know about this. What if we get caught?"

"We won't get caught," she said.

Cas thought of everything that could go wrong. Getting arrested was the biggest risk. Also, doing this would probably put him in precarious situations with the dregs of society. Buying drugs was one thing. Getting mixed up with the dealing of them was another.

It was so hard for Cas to say no to Jazzie. He'd do anything for her. It didn't take much to convince him. She essentially had him with her soft cheeks and glimmering green eyes. He was her marionette. "All right. I'll do it. I could use some extra money before I go away to college, anyway."

Jazzie's eyes grew wide, and a smile began to form on her full lips. "Really? You'll help us?"

Cas felt pretty excited at how happy he'd made Jazzie. If this is part of what it took to win her over, he'd have to take his chances.

"Yeah, I'll do it." He sucked in a breath. "I might know some people who might be interested. What's the drug?"

"It's called Nex. It's a new designer drug."

Cas shrugged. "I've never heard of it. Must be brand new."

"Oh, it is." Her smile grew bigger. "Brand spankin' new."

CHAPTER 6

SETH, AKA JERMAIN

JERMAIN DUSTED off a large yellow pages directory, sat it down on the table, and opened it up until he found the number he'd been looking for: *shipping services.*

He dialed the number. There was a long wait, a recording, and then he pressed a key on the telephone.

"Trans-Atlantic Shipping Services. Mark speaking. How may I help you?" a man with a thick New Jersey accent answered.

Jermain glanced at Colette as she paced the living room. She stopped in front of the large mirror, muttering to herself as she applied a dark lipstick, her reflection intense and focused.

"Hi, Mark. My name is Seth. I'm looking to get a quote for transporting a twenty-foot shipping container from New Jersey to the Port of St. Petersburg."

"Are you a business exporting commercial cargo or will you be relocating or moving?"

"I'll be relocating."

"Sure thing. I just have to take down some information.

What's your phone number and email address?" A rustle of paper, then, "And can I have your name again, please?"

He repeated his name and gave the man his phone number, then watched Colette as she left the room.

"My email is jermaind one-eight-five-one at a-o-l dot com."

"What's your last name, Seth?"

"It's Duran."

"When do you plan to ship your container?"

"Within the next few weeks. I'll have a more concrete date soon."

Colette returned with a flat iron. She plugged it into the wall and began to run it through her hair.

"Let's pick an arbitrary date just so I can create a more accurate quote. How does July twenty sixth sound?" the man said.

"Sure, that sounds perfect." Glancing toward Colette, he said to the man on the phone, "Sir, just a sec." He held his hand over the microphone, and to Colette, he said, "Are you going out?"

At the mirror, she flicked her eyes toward Jermain and then rolled them and shook her head. She didn't answer him and continued to straighten her hair.

"Hey, can you answer me?" he asked, his tone hardening.

Colette unplugged the flat iron and raced from the living room.

Jermain put the phone back to his ear. "I'm still here."

"All right," the man said. "I'll work on getting you a quote for a twenty-foot shipping container from Newark, New Jersey to the Great Port of Saint Petersburg and get it to you by five p.m. later today."

"Thank you so much," Jermain said.

"Take care," the man said.

Jermain hung up the phone and yelled, "Cole, where are you going?"

He heard the front door slam shut.

CHAPTER 7
THE DATE

CAS AND JAZZIE darted through the front doors of the movie theatre, running through the lobby. They dashed around a crowd of movie-goers and headed toward the box office.

Scouring the lobby, Cas caught sight of Andrew and his girlfriend, Jackie. Jackie, her arms crossed in front, sported a look of extreme annoyance.

Cas purchased two tickets for *The Day After Tomorrow* and raced to meet Andrew and Jackie, pulling Jazzie behind him.

"I'm so sorry we're late," Cas said, panting.

"We thought you weren't gonna make it!" Andrew said.

"Sorry, man!" They embraced. Cas turned towards Jackie. "Jackie, this is Jazzie," he said.

Jackie stared at Jazz, who wore a black spaghetti strap tank top over a short leather skirt. Her entire outfit was black, except for the red Gothic skull crest patch with wings on her tank. Jackie gave Jazz the kind of look a prudish spectator might give side-show performers at a carnival, frowning.

"Nice to meet you," Jackie said.

"Nice to meet you, Jackie," Jazzie said with a smile. "Hi, Andrew! Haven't seen you in a while."

"Hey!" Andrew said, sounding overly excited.

"Shall we?" Cas said.

They all continued into the dark auditorium. When they got inside, previews were playing on the screen. The movie hadn't yet started.

Cas turned to Jazzie and said, "I'm going to get some popcorn. Do you want me to get you anything?"

"I'm okay," she said, moving into an aisle seat. "Thank you."

"Jackie, we'll be right back," Andrew said. His girlfriend glared at him, but Cas grabbed his arm and tugged him away.

Cas and Andrew each ordered a large bucket of popcorn and a large soda at the concession stand.

"Her father actually let her go out on a date?" Andrew asked, his tone snarky.

"It's not her father that's the issue," Cas said. "It's her brother. I mean, we're cool and everything, but they never go anywhere without each other. I haven't met their dad. He's really sick and never leaves his bedroom. She said she doesn't want people to be near him. She's afraid he could catch something and he's in a delicate state of health."

"Damn, that's rough, man," Andrew said, grabbing two straws. "Her brother's hold on her is suffocating. He needs to chill out and let her breathe."

"Tell me about it. I wonder if she even told Seth she was going out with me tonight." Cas got his change from the cashier. "Everything seems to be so secretive with her. I ask her questions—simple questions you ask someone, and she won't tell me anything. She's a puzzle box."

"You think everything's okay at home?" Andrew asked.

Cas frowned. "What do you mean?"

"From what you've told me, things are a little strange with that family. I don't know her or her brother at all. I've only been to their place once. That one time she had some people over. It was weird there, man. It smelled kind of funky in their basement. Now that I think of it, that's why I left. It smelled like—" Andrew's brow furrowed. "Sewage. Like something toxic. I can't even explain it. It was cold in their basement, too. They're just kind of...weird. No offense, man. I know you really like her."

"Their house is old. Old houses have funky smells and drafts." Cas sighed. "Who isn't weird these days?"

"As long as you dig her and you're getting along. I guess that's all that matters."

Cas didn't respond, his mind turning over what Andrew had said. He wondered if there was something wrong with his friends, Jazzie and Seth. Sure, things were a little strange with that family, but at least strange wasn't boring, Cas thought.

"Two large popcorn and sodas," a young attendant working the concession stand called out. Cas and Andrew picked up their orders and strode back toward the auditorium.

"So did you pop her cherry yet?" Andrew asked.

"Dude. Shut up!" Cas shoved Andrew playfully. "You know I don't like talking about that stuff."

Cas flung a kernel in the air and caught it in his mouth as they went through the swinging doors.

The movie played in the dark, quiet auditorium. With a keen ear, you could almost hear the 35mm film spinning on its reel and passing through the projector. Cas glanced over at Jazzie. Her eyes were locked on the picture. He offered her some popcorn but she declined. With a gentle gesture, he slid his hand over towards hers and took it in his own.

Her fingers are so cold, Cas thought. They felt as though they'd been sitting in a cooler filled with ice.

Later that evening, Cas' car slowed to a roll in front of Jazzie's house.

This is it. If I'm ever going to make a move, it's going to be now. Cas' inner voice propelled him to act. *Kiss her. Kiss her now, you wuss!*

Cas looked over at Jazzie. Her fine gray hairs matched the moon's shimmer; her reds complemented her scarlet lipstick. A knot formed in his stomach.

"I had a really nice time tonight," he said.

He slid across the seat, his hand brushed against her breasts as he swung his arm over her head. Underneath the soft glow of the moon, Cas pressed his lips to hers. He tried with all his might not to tremble, despite his body wanting to. He felt excitement, but not like any ordinary excitement he'd ever felt before. His tongue touched hers.

Her tongue felt like a block of ice.

There was a knock on the passenger side window.

"What the fuck?" Cas pulled away from Jazzie. "Is that?"

"Shit." Jazzie turned and saw her brother outside, knocking on her window. "I'm so sorry. I have to go." Jazzie opened the car door and got out.

Seth's eyes were narrowed, their color looking almost black. His gaze followed his sister as she marched up the stairs to the porch and entered their house, all the while muttering something under his breath Cas couldn't hear.

Cas rolled down the passenger window.

"I'm sorry for interrupting, man. She was just supposed to get home a lot earlier tonight," Seth said. He crossed his arms over his chest. "We have to help our dad with something. She usually helps with his medicine."

Cas sat a little straighter, wondering if Seth was pissed about Cas kissing his sister. "It's cool. I understand... Is everything okay with your dad?"

Seth's smiled looked forced. "Yeah, he'll be all right. I've just been waiting all night for her. And she didn't tell me she was going to be home this late."

"I'm sorry," Cas stuttered. "I feel like it's my fault. We were at the movies and I guess it got late. I didn't know she—"

"Nah, nah." Seth waved his hand in the air. "No way. You're cool, man. Again, I'm sorry. She knew she had to be home early tonight."

Cas hated Seth at that moment, his nervousness gone. Why did he have to interrupt their first kiss? What was so important he had to stop them in the act? What did they have to help their father with that Seth couldn't handle on his own? Why didn't they get a home health aide? Why had he never met their father, despite having been to their house over a dozen times?

Something wasn't right. More importantly, *why was Jazzie's tongue so cold?*

CHAPTER 8

PRINCIPAL RICHARD

PRINCIPAL RICHARD'S eyes were laser focused on his computer screen when his secretary, Suzanne, stepped into his office. She closed the door behind her.

"There's a detective here to see you," she said in a whisper, her tone troubled.

His eyes widened as they panned away from the computer monitor and landed on her.

"Detective?" He swallowed the lump in his throat. "What does he want?"

She looked over her shoulder to the door, then back at him. "He wants to speak with you."

"About what?"

"I don't know." Suzanne's voice took on more urgency. "Should I let him in?"

"Yes. Yes, of course. Please, let him in."

Suzanne opened the door, stepped back out and, after a moment, ushered a tall, brawny man in his middle forties into Richard's office.

Principal Richard stood up. "Hello, Detective. How may I help you?"

The detective made his way toward Richard's desk and extended his hand.

"Hello, Principal Richard. My name is Detective Flynn. I'm with the NYPD."

"Oh?" Richard shook the offered hand, then motioned for the other man to take a seat. Then he dropped into his own chair, trying to stay calm. "To what do I owe this visit?"

"It's regarding one of your former students. Rick De Luca." Detective Flynn took out a small notepad and a pen from his jacket pocket.

Richard stared at the detective, his brain working overtime, but no words came out of his mouth.

Flynn eyed the principal. "He was a former student, right?"

"Yes. Of course." Richard swallowed hard, looking down at his desk for a moment. "We were all very saddened by his tragic death...his tragic murder." He fidgeted with his collar.

"I'm going to need a few school records, if that's all right, Principal. As you may have heard, we still haven't found the killer. It's been a week since he was murdered, and we're working overtime to find the person that did it. We'll find the killer, God willing. It may just take some more time." Flynn scanned the office.

"I've been following the case, reading the news," Richard said, "It's a shame the murderer hasn't been found yet. I hope they catch the person soon and they're brought to justice."

Flynn stared at the principal, his brow furrowed.

Richard rushed to fill the silence. "I'll get you those records—all the records we have on file for Rick—as soon as possible."

The detective scribbled in his notebook. "I appreciate

your help. Any information at this point could help us with our investigation."

Richard dialed out on his phone.

"Of course." His secretary picked up. "Suzanne, please print out all the records we have on file for Rick De Luca as soon as you can."

Detective Flynn stood up, leaned over the desk and slipped a card out of a small holder he took from his inner pocket.

"I'll wait outside in the main office. If there's anything you think of—anything you'd like to share with us that might help out our investigation, please don't hesitate to give me a call. That's my direct line." Flynn handed Principal Richard his card.

Richard took the proffered card and looked at it for a moment, trying to keep his hand from trembling. "I'll call if anything comes to mind. The records should be ready in just a few minutes."

"Thank you for your time, Richard."

"It's my pleasure. Anything I can do to help." He felt relief wash over him the closer the man got to the door. "Good luck with the investigation. I hope they catch the killer soon."

Just before leaving the office, Flynn stopped at the door, turned and pointed to a large oil painting over an antique credenza. The subject was a priest delivering the Eucharist in an old medieval church. The detective stared at it for a few seconds and said, "Beautiful painting," before continuing out of the office.

CHAPTER 9

THE PLAN

COLETTE STORMED into her bedroom and slammed the door behind her. She slid the latch, locking the door.

She heard heavy footfalls approach the other side of the door.

"Open up!" Jermain said, banging fiercely on the door.

"Leave me alone!"

"What the fuck was that? You're kissing him? That's not part of the plan." He banged the door with angry fists. "Open up so we can talk about this."

She walked across the room and studied the darkness beyond her window. "I don't want to talk about it!"

"Open this damned door right now! You have no idea what you're doing!"

"You're right. I don't know what I'm doing!" she wailed. "I've been doing everything you say forever... I follow all your instructions. What if this doesn't even work? What if his blood doesn't save Father?"

"What other option do we have?" Jermain stopped banging on the door, and his voice lowered to a more uniform, even volume. "You remember what Alexandru said. Either we give Dad more of Şerban's blood, which is impossible because we killed him, or we give him Casimir's blood. Remember how difficult it was to find a young saint. Casimir's blood is the youngest and the freshest. And Şerban would've come back by now—we would've crossed paths with him—if he were still alive. We have to try." Jermain's words tumbled out, a jumble of frenzy and wild hope fighting against the heavy weight of his desperation. "I've started building the shipping container. It'll be ready by next week. We'll be able to leave soon."

Colette went over to her door and slid the latch open. Jermain stormed into the bedroom and grasped her neck, choking her until her feet lifted off the ground.

"Kissing our saint isn't part of the plan," Jermain yelled, his eyes blazing. "What the hell's gotten into you?"

Colette gripped Jermain's hands, attempting to pry them off her neck.

"Technically, he's not a saint. He's a descendant of a saint," she said through her bruised throat.

Jermain hurled her onto her futon like a doll. She landed on her back and sat upright, rubbing at her neck.

"When will we be leaving?" she asked.

"We can leave as soon as the container is ready. I'm having it built at a warehouse in Long Island City. The exporter will pick it up there and truck it over to Newark. We'll be leaving from there. We should leave soon." Jermain gave Colette a grave look. "The media won't stop reporting on Rick's murder. I didn't think it would become a major news story." Jermain bit his lips, leaving ruby droplets on the torn skin. "They could be on to us. New York police officers are sharp."

"How long will it take to get to Russia? We're going to Saint Petersburg, right?"

He nodded. "Yeah. It'll take thirty-three days. Twenty-three days to Copenhagen, Denmark. From there, our container will get transported to another ship that takes us to Saint Petersburg. That'll be another ten days. We'll be safe when we get there. We can live there forever. And hopefully—"

"Hopefully, Dad will be cured," Colette said.

Jermain sat beside her on the futon.

"You're not starting to have feelings for Casimir, are you?" He laid a hand over hers. "Have you two been spending a lot of time together?"

"No." She looked away. "He's cute, but I know what needs to be done."

"He is cute." Jermain laughed. "He's going to be even cuter when we give Father his miracle blood."

Colette frowned. "Are we going to turn him?"

"Maybe we can. Eventually."

Silence.

"If Father gets better. We have to wait and see if his blood is the cure, first. We can't risk tainting it." Jermain looked over at her, his expression troubled. "Would you like him to join our family?"

"I don't know. Maybe. It might be a nice idea."

CHAPTER 10

THE EXPORTER

THE FORKLIFT MOTORED up the wooden ramp and into the shipping container as the operator expertly balanced and maneuvered a porta potty on the forks. Steering with care, the operator lowered the porta potty into the back corner of the container.

Jermain stood at the entrance of the container, observing the work in progress. The shipping container was nearly ready. Fiberglass had been installed inside the container walls, layered with rubber foam to ensure the container would be soundproof. There was a TV mounted on another side of the container, equipped with a DVD player. A little entertainment for their thirty-three-day voyage at sea. A portable bathtub was secured to the floor on one side of the container. Even vampires had to bathe. An eighteen-cubic-foot chest freezer was secured to another end of the container's floor. Inside the freezer, they'd pack bags of blood for their journey, for Casimir's blood would be reserved for their father. They needed to arrive in Russia with ample energy, so they figured saint blood, plus fifty gallons of blood ration would suffice their thirst.

"Carlos," Jermain said, signaling the man using the machine.

The forklift operator, Carlos, wore headphones and didn't hear Jermain's voice. He backed out of the shipping container.

"HEY, CARLOS!" Jermain jumped around, waving his arms to get the man's attention.

Carlos took off his headphones and smiled at Jermain.

"What do you think so far?"

"It looks amazing!" Jermain knew the shipping container would be just what they needed for their journey. "I can't believe how quickly you've done all this."

"They don't call me Carlos, *The Man,* for no reason," Carlos said, laughing at his own joke.

"When do you think it'll be ready?"

"I'll have it ready in the next few days."

Carlos drove his forklift back down the rampart. It didn't happen often, but a glint of a smile formed on Jermain's face.

Upon returning to the house, once inside the foyer, Jermain heard Colette yelling from the second floor.

"Oh, God, no! Please." Her frantic tone scared him.

He raced up the stairs and entered their father's bedroom. His sister sat next to the bed, hysterical. Colette's hands were over her face, her eyes soaked in blood.

She raised her head as Jermain entered. "He won't wake up. I tried to feed him, but I couldn't get him to wake up!"

"Fuck." Jermain stared down at his father. His eyes were closed and he looked paler than usual, like an old corpse, decomposing before their eyes.

"What do we do?" Colette asked.

"What did you try to feed him?"

She gestured to a box next to the bed. "A cat."

"Dammit! You know he doesn't like cat," Jermain said angrily. "We need to get him a human, fast. Can you go out and find one?"

"Now?" Colette asked.

"No, tomorrow. When he's fucking dead," Jermain cried. "Yes, now!"

Colette stormed out of the room, hurried down the stairs and slammed the front door on her way out.

Jermain bit his wrist and held it over his father's face. He forced his father's mouth open and tilted his arm to allow the blood to drizzle into his mouth.

Nothing happened.

Jermain pried open his father's eyelids.

"Dad, wake up!" He smacked his father's face lightly. "Don't die on us. Please, wake up." Jermain bit his wrist again, this time very deep, and an ichor of blood oozed from his veins. He funneled as much blood as he could directly into his father's mouth. Jermain grew woozy. He'd released too much of his blood, too quickly, and his feet couldn't hold him upright any longer. The young vampire toppled over, collapsing into onto his father's coffin, almost knocking it over.

Jermain's eyelids flickered as he heard the front door open. There was a loud thud downstairs, like a bowling ball being dropped on the wooden floor.

"I need help, Jermain! Come down, please!"

Jermain picked himself off the floor and made his way down the stairs and saw Colette hunched on the bench in the foyer, panting heavily. A small woman with wiry gray hair lay on the floor near the foot of the stairs. She twitched, her blue eyes blankly staring towards Jermain, as blood pooled near the base of her head.

"I think I broke her back," Colette said. "I had to carry her a few blocks. She looks small, but she's heavy. She put up a good fight," Colette said sounding out of breath.

"You couldn't find anyone younger?" Jermain said, frowning as he reached the foyer level.

Colette shook her head, looking angry. "There weren't many people outside. I brought back what I could find."

Jermain hurried over and picked the woman up from behind, hoisting her under her arms. He shook his head in disgust as his face touched her greasy hair. She was a solid little barrel of a woman. Jermain was much stronger than his sister, but even the small woman's weight surprised him.

"You weren't kidding. What does she have, bricks for organs?"

He hauled her up the stairs and dragged her down the hallway to their father's bedroom. Once inside, Jermain pierced her neck with his fangs. Blood hemorrhaged in all directions, gushing onto the coffin and the carpet. As strategically as he could, he positioned the woman's neck over Charles' mouth. Much of the blood was wasted, spilling onto Charles' face and neck and getting lost in his coffin. Jermain grabbed a chalice from a nearby table and collected the woman's blood, then poured a good measure —as much as he could accumulate—into his father's mouth. Charles began to gurgle as the blood flowed into his system. *Regurgitation is good,* Jermain thought. *Means he's still kickin'.*

The doorbell rang, echoing up the stairs.

What now?

"Dad, I'll be right back." He patted his dad's forehead.

"Cole, can you get the door?" Jermain yelled down to his sister. "Check to see who it is first."

Jermain made his way down the stairs and saw his sister still sitting on the bench near the stairs, hunched over in the same position he'd left her a few minutes before, clutching her stomach.

"You okay?"

Colette looked up, grimacing. She moved her hand and arm away from her stomach. A long knife hilt protruded from her gut.

"What the hell? You got stabbed?" Jermain couldn't believe what he was seeing. And she hadn't said anything.

She raised her head to look at him. "Yeah," she said with a cough.

Jermain could scarcely hear her. "The woman?"

Colette nodded.

"Goddamn it!"

Jermain strode over toward his sister and examined the knife. He dropped to one knee.

"This might hurt."

He gripped the knife handle and removed it in one swift motion.

Dark blood flowed from a small hole near her navel. Jermain raised her shirt to examine the wound; it resembled a midline incision on her belly.

She placed her hand back on her stomach, covering the wound, and blood began to flow from her eyes.

"Why does life have to be so difficult?" she asked, crying now.

The doorbell rang again.

"ONE MINUTE," he all but screamed, then turned back to his sister. I'll get something to wrap it with."

Jermain hurried to the downstairs bathroom and found

medical cloth and gauze tape. He ran back up and patched Colette's stomach. Once he had finished, he went to the front door and looked through the viewfinder.

"Who is it?" he asked.

"Hi. My name is Beth. I live next door," a woman said from the other side of the door. "I heard some noise and I just wanted to check to see if everything is all right in there... I'm sorry, I don't think we've officially met."

"Yeah, everything is fine," Jermain answered, his arm resting on the door. He dropped his head and let it rest on his arm for support for a moment before going on. "My sister fell, but she's okay. Sorry I can't talk right now, but thanks for checking on us." He turned and returned to where his sister lay on the bench, clutching her tape and gauze. The blood had already soaked through the gauze.

"I'm fine!" Colette yelled, then winced as if raising her voice had sent pain to her midsection.

"All right. Let me know if you ever need anything," the woman said, her voice fading as he heard her steps moving away from the door. Jermain hoped she could just mind her own damned business and not call the police or anything.

Jermain caressed his sister's hair. "I'm going to go check on Dad."

"Okay," Colette said, staring down sadly. "I'm sorry, Jermain. I'm really sorry." Her words sounded more hope-less than apologetic.

Jermain said nothing. He gazed at his sister for a few more seconds, then shuffled up the stairs to tend to Charles. His sister would be all right. A dagger wound wouldn't kill her. They were vampires and it would take a lot more to kill either of them. Perhaps a stake through the heart coupled with conflagration of the body. That might do the trick.

Even then, Jermain thought, it'd be difficult to end the vampire's life.

Though the dagger wound didn't pose a fatal risk, it had a certain other connotation. It was an omen, pure and simple. Jermain carried his sister and his father on his back, at times, almost literally. Tonight's events made him nervous. He felt as though things were beginning to come undone. Entropy, he thought, was a force even vampires could not evade. More alarmingly, Jermain sensed the authorities closing in on them. His mind flashed with images of police officers, firearms, canine units, and flash-bangs. He'd had these premonitions in the past, and more often than not, they were accurate. They would have to speed up their plans and come up with a large sum of money quickly if they were to succeed.

CHAPTER 11

GHOSTS

THE FLUORESCENT LIGHTS inside the one hundred and fourth precinct cast shadows on Detective Patrick Flynn's desk as he rubbed the back of his neck. He looked at the clock on the wall. It was nine-forty-seven p.m. This case was all blurs and shadows, Flynn thought.

Two hundred and seventy-eight murders had already been committed throughout New York City that year and it was only June. By the end of the year, he estimated there'd be at least another five hundred and fifty or more killings. This case, Flynn thought, was not only clouded in an opaque veil, but it could possibly lead to something else, something bigger. It was a hunch he'd developed having been on the force for more than thirteen years. Intuition had taught Flynn good things happened when he followed his hunches, so that was his modus operandi.

A female officer, Amanda Diaz, carrying a tactical duffle bag and dressed in plain clothes stopped at his desk. Flynn thought she looked more tired than he felt.

"Are you burning the midnight oil tonight, Flynn?" she asked.

He took a sip from his cold coffee and ran a hand through his dark hair.

"Something isn't right," he said, picking up the file on his desk and weighing it in his hands, wondering why it was so thin on information.

"What isn't right?"

"I can't find any information on any of them."

"On who?"

"Exactly." He let the word hang for a few seconds. "That's exactly my problem."

"You need me to run any more reports on those teenagers?" she asked. "I've got no problem running some more."

"I've run everything I could. They're like ghosts. They don't exist," Flynn said. "My guess is they're from a different country. But their English is *too* good. It just doesn't add up."

"Maybe sleep on it. You'll find what you're looking for in time." She gave him a reassuring smile.

Flynn nodded, then leaned back in his chair and placed his hands behind his head.

"You coming in tomorrow?" he asked.

"You know it," she said, giving him a two-fingered salute as she turned to leave.

"Have a good night, Diaz."

The next morning, Flynn stood in the station's briefing room, handing a small team of officers a one-sheet to study. "I've put out requests for every type of report through government databases and have been unable to obtain any information regarding Jazzie, Seth, or their father," Flynn said. "I only know about their father because I've heard them refer to him in the recordings. Apparently, the man is bedridden and never leaves the home."

The officers listened intently.

"The whole thing is just strange," Flynn continued. "Their names—at least the ones they use—their addresses, birth records, none of it is on any government databases. They're ghosts. The only information anyone has on any of them are their first names—Seth, Jazzie, and their father, who they refer to as *Dad*, or *Father*," Flynn said. "It's like they just appeared out of nowhere."

"How long have they been at that address?" an officer in the front asked.

"A little over a year," Flynn said.

"Who owns the house? They're renting, right?" the same officer asked.

Flynn flipped open a file that sat on his desk. "It's an LLC. Appears to be a shell corp. I haven't found an owner yet," Flynn said, looking back up at the officers in the room. "The whole thing reeks of bad juju. I'm not entirely sure, but I have a gut feeling this could be cult-related. I just need to connect some more dots."

"Did you request a warrant yet?" Another officer asked. "What's holding you back?"

"I'm working on it," Flynn said. "But I don't want to go in just yet. Aside from the drug they're pushing, I think they're involved in other crimes."

The officer leaned forward, frowning. "Yeah? Like what?

Detective Flynn turned and stared at the whiteboard. In the center was a picture of Rick De Luca, and a web connecting him to others had been drawn. The names of faculty and students from Saint Thomas Prep were listed: Principal Richard, Casimir Jaworski, and a few others.

There were also fuzzy photographs of Jazzie and Seth taken at night, and in parentheses next to their names, the word "alias."

After a short silence, Flynn said, "I think they could somehow be tied to the Vampire Murders."

"You think they're connected to Rick De Luca's murder?" an officer asked, raising her brow.

"The witness at Grove Park, the one who saw Rick De Luca the night he was murdered, mentioned a young blonde male walking a trail about twenty minutes before Rick was murdered," Flynn said. "The witness guessed he was anywhere from seventeen to twenty-one years old. That fits Seth's description. We have two other witnesses who have come forward claiming they've seen a young girl, possibly between fifteen and nineteen, with red hair, near the crime scenes of a couple of the other Vampire Murders."

That night, Detective Flynn, sitting in an unmarked police car, peered through binoculars at a second-floor window of Jazzie and Seth's home. The shades were pulled down, but a flickering light still shone through. *Candles perhaps?* The light went off moments later.

Thirty minutes after that, a lanky teenager emerged from around the house. Flynn, stirring from a half-sleep, peered into his binoculars. The teen, wearing a backpack and carrying two medium-sized duffle bags, loaded them into a black Honda Civic parked a few spaces away.

"Casimir," Flynn whispered to himself, recalling the young man's name and face from his whiteboard.

The Honda's engine rumbled to life, and the car drove away.

———

A single lamp on the wall cast a circle of yellow light, illuminating a large map spread out on the table before them. Jermain stood over it, his hands clasped behind his back, his posture as rigid as a military general poring over a battle plan. He pointed to a small, winding line drawn across the paper with a pen.

"We depart from Newark, New Jersey and sail up the North Atlantic Ocean, crossing to the English Channel. Once we pass through the English Channel, we'll enter the North Sea and continue north from thereon." Jermain pointed to the line on the map. "Here, the ship will pass through the Skagerrak Strait, which separates Norway and Denmark, then enter and continue through the Kattegat Strait until we arrive in Copenhagen. There we'll be transferred to the second ship."

"How long does the transfer take?"

"We head out on the following day after arriving in Copenhagen. Once on route again, the ship will pass through the Øresund Strait until we enter the Baltic Sea. After the Baltic Sea, the ship will sail through the Gulf of Finland until our arrival in Saint Petersburg, where we'll dock. From there I've arranged a truck to take us to a small town two and a half hours east from Saint Petersburg."

Colette looked up at him. "Thirty-three days?"

"Yes. Thirty-three days if all goes according to plan." Jermain saw the worry on her face. "Don't worry, Cole. It's going to work."

NEX

CASIMIR SAT at his small desk, browsing the internet, when his cell phone rang. He didn't recognize the number and wondered if he should answer it. He hesitated for a moment, then answered. "Hello?"

"Yo, it's Mike. Where you been? I been tryin' to call you all day."

Crazy Mike, the guy who was spearheading most of the distribution and sale of Nex, was on the line.

Cas stood up from his chair. "I was at school. What's up, man? I didn't recognize this number."

"I'm calling from a payphone..." Mike sounded out of breath, his tone urgent. "Yo, I got some bad news."

"What is it?"

"That stuff we've been pushin'..."

Silence.

"Yeah?" Casimir clenched his jaw.

"I just talked to my guy. Four kids died from it." Mike sighed. "What the fuck is that stuff, man? What's in it?"

"I don't know. My connect didn't tell me. She just said it's a new—"

"I'm done with this shit," Mike interrupted. "I don't want any more blood on my hands.

I'm done, man. You hear me?" His voice rose. "I'm out," he cried, clicking off the line.

Casimir just stood there, the dead phone in his hand. He didn't sleep that night. He tossed and turned and sweat profusely until he dragged himself out of his bed and took a cold shower. The weight of the teenage lives lost through his negligence ate at his consciousness like a school of piranha. Thanks to stupidity and greed, people had died. This was not what he'd envisioned when he'd agreed to help out Jazzie and Seth. He felt like they'd deceived him. Did they know what sort of drug Nex was, and how dangerous it was? Casimir felt like a complete fool. The guilt made him feel sick and disgusted and rotten. That night, he kneeled beside his bed and did something he hadn't done since he was twelve. He prayed to God for forgiveness.

———

The next morning, Detective Flynn stared at the whiteboard in the briefing office. He could feel the dark, puffy rings under his sleep-deprived eyes, the result of weeks with very little rest. He wanted to make a break in the case, and the only way to accomplish that, he figured, was to put in the work.

On the whiteboard, he saw an intricate web of potential suspects and deceased persons potentially related to the Vampire Murders. Below the web, two columns had been drawn—one for vampire deaths and another for drug deaths.

Another detective entered the office. The other man pointed toward one of the columns, and said, "You're going to have to update that. We're already up to eight deaths this week. We're thinking it was a tainted batch of fentanyl that got around."

Flynn rubbed out the number for drug deaths—fourteen. With a dry-erase marker, he wrote the number twenty-two.

The other detective continued: "Traces of LSD have been found in the victims' bodies. According to the medical examiner, they're also finding high doses of fentanyl and are classifying the cause of death as a drug overdose." He handed Flynn a file.

Flynn opened the file and sifted through pages of typed reports and photographs. His brow raised. "Do we have any leads on where this stuff is coming from?" he asked, meeting the other man's gaze.

"We questioned one kid who actually survived an overdose. He was with the group of four that died. He's talking," the detective said. "He told us where he got it from. We've put out a warrant already and the team's on it."

"Where's that information?"

The detective pointed to a page in the file. Flynn's eyes widened. *Bingo,* he thought. *Casimir Jaworski.*

An hour later, Detective Flynn rang the bell to Casimir's apartment. Behind him stood two stone-faced narcotics detectives. A middle-aged woman answered the door, opening it only slightly, the door secured with a chain.

"Who is it?" the woman asked, her voice nervous, brown eyes peering through the gap.

"My name is Detective Flynn. I'm with the NYPD."

"How can I help you?"

"We're looking for Casimir Jaworski, miss. Is he home?"

"He's not home at the moment."

"Are you his mother? Do you know where he went?"

"Can I see some IDs?" she asked.

Detective Flynn and the other officers showed their badges through the opening.

She unhooked the chain and opened the door.

"I am his mother. What's this about?"

"May we come in, Mrs. Jaworski? Your son may have gotten himself in some trouble."

She hesitated for a moment, but allowed them inside. She guided them into the small apartment and motioned toward the couch.

"Cas left late last night and I haven't heard from him since," she said, pulling a chair from the dining table to face the detectives. She sat down, her hands nervously wringing a napkin. Flynn wondered if she had any idea what her son had gotten himself into.

"Are his friends Jazzie and Seth?" Flynn asked.

"Jazzie's his new girlfriend. They've been hanging out now for a few months. He might be staying over at her house..." She paused, observing the detective carefully. "He's seventeen, going on eighteen in a few months. I don't feel the need to ask him where he's going every time he leaves the apartment." She sighed. "Does that make me a bad mother?"

"Do you know his friends? Jazzie and Seth?"

"I've only met Jazzie once. I gave him a ride over to her place when his car was at the shop. I met her briefly, only spoke to her for a minute, if that. She seemed like a nice girl. Dressed kinda quirky, but I didn't see anything mean about her." She opened her mouth as if to speak, then stopped, then went on. "She wears a gorgeous necklace. It looks like something that might've been passed down to her from her grandmother—an antique."

"We're aware of her necklace. It was included in a description we got from an eye-witness that tied her to a couple of crimes," Flynn said.

"What has my son gotten himself into? What crimes?" she asked, raising a hand up to her mouth.

"I'm not at liberty to say, Mrs. Jaworski. It's still an ongoing investigation. But I'm sure you can help us out by providing us some information." Detective Flynn looked at her gravely. "Mrs. Jaworski...your son has gotten involved with some *very* bad people. We need to locate him, and do so as soon as possible."

"What do you mean by very bad people? What did they do?"

"We have reason to believe these people—the young girl and her family—are involved in very serious crimes, and we have some evidence that your son has gotten himself mixed up with them."

"Oh, my. Let me try to call him again. He hasn't been picking up." She stood and grabbed her phone. Her hands slightly shaky, she fumbled with the device, then dialed. She seemed to let it ring several times. "It's going straight to voicemail," she said, dropping the phone and beginning to cry. "It isn't like him to spend a night away and not call the next day," she sobbed. "I don't want anything to happen to my baby! Where is he? I haven't seen him since last night. Can you help me find him?"

She keeled over and collapsed in the dining room as the tears flooded onto the timeworn linoleum.

Detective Flynn went over to her, putting an arm around her shoulders. He gently patted her back, a helpless gesture for a mother who, he feared, had just lost her son. "We're looking for him. We're doing everything we can, Mrs. Jaworski. We're working with the FBI, and other agencies are assisting as well."

He hated this part of the job. The part where he had to console parents, loved ones, who might have just lost a child. He felt compelled to lie and tell them everything was going to be okay.

"Where's my baby? Where's Casimir?" she wailed.

"We're going to find him," Flynn said, gently rubbing the woman's back.

CHAPTER 13

THE VOYAGE

VOYAGE NIGHT 1

JERMAIN HAD TRANSLOCATED and was crouching on top of a nearby shipping container. He wore a long, flowing cloak with a high collar, but its thin material offered little warmth, and he shuddered. With keen eyes, he watched the massive cargo ship cut through the icy North Atlantic. A fierce gale made the waters rough, and the wind slapped hard against his face as he gazed into the darkness. There weren't any crew members nearby; he'd made sure of that before perching so visibly out in the open. Most were asleep, and the few tasked with making early morning rounds were on the opposite side of the ship at the moment.

Jermain scanned the cargo containers stacked like massive Lego pieces along the ship as it churned through the gray sea. He wondered how his sister was holding up. The plan was their only chance at a new start—if Casimir's blood was the remedy their father needed. *It has to work,* Jermain thought, his gut tightening. They'd come this far and they'd put all their eggs in one basket. There was no turning back.

————

Inside the container, under the murky oxidized-colored light, Colette gave Casimir more Nex—a mixture of modified lysergic acid and fentanyl. One drop of the narcotic would teleport a user to another universe. Fearing Casimir might rebel, she'd given him a full syringe of the substance, hoping it would leave him disoriented and docile, though she worried too much might be fatal. It was a difficult balance, and she was neither a chemist nor a doctor. They needed to draw his blood for their father, but not have him wake up and see what they were doing to him.

Colette felt a lot of guilt over the whole scheme. They had initially planned to leave at the end of August, but Jermain had noticed a suspicious car parked across the street from their home. After some research, he tied the car to Detective Flynn. He'd been getting strong visions of authorities closing in on them and had even found proof they were being monitored. So, they decided to speed up their timeline.

She'd invited Cas to a party the night they kidnapped him. It was a Friday night. Casimir was on summer vacation and she'd convinced him over to her house first, telling him they could pregame there, then head on out to the shindig. Upon his arrival, she'd slipped Casimir a bit of Nex, and the next time he opened his eyes, they were all on board the ship.

Colette glanced at him as he lay, sunken in the couch. She wondered if he had any idea where he was, or if he thought he was still at her house. His eyes appeared glazed over, taking in his surroundings. *Poor kid is lost in some other universe,* Colette thought.

Jermain was rummaging near the television, checking underneath all the furniture and inside their luggage. He sighed, then turned to her and said, "You were supposed to pack the DVDs. Did you pack them?"

She groaned. "Damn it! I forgot."

"You couldn't handle packing a few things, could you? I guess all we have to watch is *The Mummy.* Good thing I brought the PlayStation with a few games. Thanks for forgetting all our movies as we embark on a month-long voyage across the Atlantic."

"I'm sorry," she said. "I was too focused on getting a hold of Cas and making sure no one saw me. Sorry for forgetting the stupid DVDs!"

He held up a CD case holder. "And good thing I brought my music. At least we'll have something to listen to." He glided toward the stereo, and fed the CD into the disk holder. As the heavy metal music blared from the speakers, he bobbed his head and cranked the dial up to concert level decibels.

VOYAGE NIGHT 2

Colette tied a rubber band around Cas' right arm, forming a tourniquet. She inserted a needle near the crook of his elbow and collected his blood into five vials. Cas' skin looked pale and clammy; his eyes were glazed over; he looked like he was lost in a fog.

"How are you feeling?" she asked softly.

He moved his lips feebly but didn't respond, appearing to have lost control of his motor functions.

"Are you able to move?" She bent down to plant a light kiss on his cheek. "If you need anything, just let me know."

Casimir closed his eyes and sank into the couch, which would serve as his bed for the duration of the voyage.

No matter how hard she tried, she could not read Casimir's mind. She fixed her eyes on him, inhaled deeply, and focused. *Mmmmmmmmmmm.* She attempted to read it again. Nothing. His thoughts were blocked. Cas' mind was a burglary safe, and no matter how hard she tried, she couldn't figure out the combination. His was the only human mind she'd ever encountered whose thoughts she wasn't able to penetrate. Jermain had also tried but was equally unsuccessful.

Colette glanced over at their father, who, just a few feet away, lay in his coffin in a profound slumber. She brought over the vials and injected Casimir's blood into her father's arm. She studied his face closely, her mind racing. *How long will it take for him to get better? What will he be like once the saint blood begins to take effect?*

She and Jermain had spent decades getting to this point, and they had scoured archives, libraries, and courthouses for a solution. Churches were impossible; stepping into one would harm or even kill them. But through a stroke of luck, they found that Casimir Jaworski was a direct descendant of Saint Casimir of Poland. He was born on October 3rd, the very same day as the saint, five hundred and twenty-eight years later. If what Şerban had told them was true, then Casimir would be their best chance at fixing their father.

In their digging, Colette and Jermain had found other descendants, but many were clustered in Europe, Africa, and South America. And from the records they found, most of these other prospects were elderly. One descendant, in particular, who lived in Chile, was ninety-seven years old. The siblings were skeptical, figuring an older person's blood might not be as effective as a younger person's. So, they rolled the dice and went with the younger descendant—the lucky winner—Casimir Jaworski.

VOYAGE NIGHT 5

"Dad...dad," Colette said, trying to shake him awake. She injected Casimir's blood into a vein in Charles' left arm. "Dad, are you awake?"

Nothing.

She shook him gently.

"He still sleeps most of the night and all day," Jermain said.

They stared with bitterness at the corpse-like creature that at one point in time resembled their father.

"Maybe Casimir's blood just needs more time," Colette said, taking a deep breath and hoping he would stir. "His system is still absorbing it."

She gazed at Jermain, who was scowling through narrowed eyes. It had been five days since they began injecting their dad with saint blood, and there was still no progress. *What if everything we've worked for doesn't work?*

she thought, a sick lump of dread tightening in her stomach. They had risked everything to get here, and there was no turning back. They would have to keep trying.

VOYAGE NIGHT 7

On the seventh day, the colossal cargo ship lurched aggressively as it cut through the increasingly turbulent waters. Inside the cargo container, Colette grabbed the loveseat to keep herself from falling. They were now somewhere very far north in the Atlantic.

She unwrapped an individual meal pack, the kind military personnel eat, and fed it to Cas. His right arm was hooked into an IV vitamin drip. Since they had been continually draining him of blood, Jermain claimed the IV would assist in his recovery. She also fed Cas additional vitamin supplements in an attempt to ensure his health stayed strong. They couldn't risk him or his blood becoming weak.

Cas attempted to stand but his legs gave out in seconds, and he plopped back down onto the couch.

"What are you doing?" Colette asked, moving closer.

He looked like he was moving his lips, but no sounds came out. He tried to stand again, but he teetered, his legs moving like jelly.

"Sit back down," she said, placing him back on the couch and covering him with a fleece blanket. Despite the container's insulation, the chilly winds of the North Atlantic still managed to creep in.

Colette shivered. She saw Cas tremble and hug his blanket. She glanced at the television. *The Mummy* was playing again—their only movie.

She patted his head and told him, "This is a good one."

On the television, Brendan Fraser tossed a stick of dynamite and dove out of harm's way. The blast obliterated a group of mummies. Colette smiled; it was one of her favorite movies.

Jermain went over to the stereo and turned the music up louder. The heavy metal rattled throughout the container. Cas pressed his hands to his ears and grimaced, his eyes closed as though he were suffering silently and in a great deal of pain. Colette patted his hair and whispered, "Everything is going to be okay."

VOYAGE NIGHT 10

Colette flung open the fourteen cubic foot freezer that had been secured to the container's floor, and regarded the neatly packed blood bags inside.

Dinner time, she told herself. She counted the remaining bags—they were down to twenty-two. She pulled one from the freezer and returned to the futon, sitting closely next to Casimir.

She snuggled up close to him. "I'm going to tell you a story," she said, caressing his shoulder and laying her head on his chest. "There was once a magical boat that sailed through the beautiful sky all the way from the East to the far West, bringing light and heat to shine down on all the world."

Colette paused to gluttonously suck on the bag, her mouth making loud slurping sounds. Her lips glistened red with blood as she inhaled half of it in a few seconds.

The cargo ship rocked aggressively.

Cas turned his head and faced her. He was trying to say something. She raised her head so her ear was close to his mouth.

"What's that, honey?" she asked.

"Where are we?" he whispered. "Where are you taking me?"

She smiled. "Don't worry, sweetie. You don't have to worry," she said, patting his head gently. "We're going somewhere safe. And pretty soon, you'll be a part of our family."

Casimir's head fell back and his eyes closed.

Colette attempted to ignore how sickly he looked. It looked as though the voyage was getting to him. He was human, after all—a mortal. But she wouldn't let herself accept that there was a real possibility he could die on their journey. She sat close to him and rested her head back on his chest.

A wild fantasy entered her mind. If her brother weren't sitting ten feet away, she would take off her and Cas' clothes and have sex with him, right then and there on the couch. She had grown to really like him. She would never admit that to her brother, but she suspected he knew. Jermain was no dummy; he'd seen them kissing that time in the car in front of their Queens home. The problem was, she couldn't have sex with him. She couldn't risk it. Casimir had to remain a virgin. Jermain had discussed this with her already, and she took her brother's commands very seriously. Since Casimir had saint blood and was a virgin, his blood was the most immaculate. Besides, she had never performed the act herself. *Can vampires even have sex with mortals? What would happen if I tried?*

In just under twenty-three days, they'd reach freedom in Russia. And by then their father would be well again. If all went according to plan, Charles' powers would be rejuvenated in just a little over three weeks' time. Her lips curled into a loose and giddy grin. The blood she drank tasted delicious. She looked down at Cas, envisioning the bliss they would both experience once he was turned into one of them. He'd be her future husband, she thought, once he was officially a vampire. *We could have a small ceremony. Wouldn't that be lovely?*

She thought of all the sacrifices she and her brother had made for their father, for themselves, and for their future. Good things were coming to them. Finally, life would be as joyful again as it was when she was a little girl, back when they were a happy family living off Rampart Street in their cozy mansion.

The massive cargo ship rolled turbulently. Colette lurched into Casimir. Cas pointed toward a bucket at the base of the couch, as if begging her to bring it closer. She retrieved it quickly and placed it next to him. He folded toward it and began to vomit.

VOYAGE NIGHT 13

"Nothing's happening!" Jermain fumed, pacing back and forth, his eyes turning blood red. "I don't understand. Alexandru said this would work. Why isn't Dad getting any better?"

Colette didn't immediately respond. She glanced over at her father, who lay in his coffin with his eyes closed tightly like a corpse in a morgue. There had been no visible change in his appearance compared to the onset of their voyage. He appeared as he did before—a sickly, pale, decaying wax figure, a mere wisp of the man Colette had known when he was a mortal. He was a distant echo of himself, a cold imitation of her father. At least back then he would occasionally talk with her and Jermain. Now it seemed they were caring for a corpse.

"Do you think he lied to us?" she asked, her face rigid, her lips tight.

"I'm not sure. He sounded sincere," Jermain said. "He sounded like he knew what he was talking about. He told us about how a small amount of saint blood was used to revive an injured vampire back in the fifteenth century. He spoke about Vlad."

"He could've been lying to us! How could we have trusted him? He attacked you. He almost killed you!" Colette cried.

"He was angry that we had killed his brother. I think if he wanted to, he could've easily killed me. He may have been trying to teach me a lesson. My fangs grew back after two months." Jermain looked over at Casimir, who lay sprawled on the couch, unconscious and twitching. "Don't give him any more Nex. The amount you've been giving him—don't be surprised if you end up killing him. He isn't any use to us as a dead boy."

"What if he wakes up?"

"If he wakes up and realizes where he is then we'll just have to restrain him. But stop giving him so much of that junk." Jermain's arms were crossed. He gave Colette a reproving glance. "You're going to kill him if you keep giving him that stuff." He looked over again at Casimir and hoped that his blood would do something for their father. Anything. Worry gnawed at him as he watched the glistening sweat drip from Casimir's forehead, despite the container feeling like an icebox.

VOYAGE NIGHT 20

"We're going to be in Copenhagen soon and he hasn't gotten up," Colette said.

Jermain was focused on his car racing video game while Colette took quick, anxious tokes from a joint. She didn't do drugs often, but the anxiety had really gotten to her. Despite her compulsion to find relief, the marijuana only seemed to make her more nervous.

She paced to her father's coffin and back toward the end of the container, the smoke from the joint billowing throughout the cramped confines. She took more anxious tokes, her fingers trembling as she glanced at Jermain, who sat in his chair, muttering to himself.

"Maybe we need to draw his blood the old way," Jermain said.

"You think that would make a difference? What if we harm him?"

"Well, what we've been doing hasn't been working, so I don't know what else to do." His fingers tapped and fiddled with the joystick as he concentrated on his game.

Colette rummaged through a medicine bag reserved for Casimir. She took out a small plastic bottle, unscrewed the top, and fished out a pill. "Cas, it's time for your medicine," she said as she nestled beside him on the couch. They'd been giving him coagulants to keep his blood from clotting, but despite all the medication, Cas seemed to be fading fast. His eyes were closed, and he hadn't been moving much the last few days. When his eyes were open, Colette thought by his stare that he was slipping away.

A bucket lay on the floor near Cas' feet. He'd been sick for several days and hadn't left the couch since day eleven of their voyage.

"He's in a torpid state," Colette said. "Do you think we should stop draining him for a few days and let him recuperate?"

"It's been twenty days, Cole. It would have worked by now!" Jermain sprang from his chair, went over to the side of the container, and slammed his fist against the metal wall.

The boom rattled the container and left Colette's ears ringing.

Cas began to mumble something and then stood up from the couch.

"He's awake," Jermain said.

Colette glanced at Cas as he wobbled in place. His pupils looked constricted and his eyes appeared bloodshot red and inflamed.

"What is it, sweetie?" She moved in closer. "Do we need to let you rest?"

She pressed her ear next to his mouth, straining to read his thoughts. Still, nothing. Then, through a scarcely audible mumble, Colette heard Casimir say, "...my feet."

"What about your feet?"

Cas rubbed his back underneath his shirt and grimaced.

"Is it your back or your feet? Which one is it, sweetheart?"

Cas groaned, his eyes unable to stay open for more than a few seconds. He teetered and tottered in place, balancing on legs that had wasted away over the last twenty days. Colette lay him down on the couch face-first. She raised his shirt and inspected his back. Her eyes opened wide as she saw discolored patches of red and white all over his skin, with deep, oozing bedsores spread across his lower back and down to his buttocks.

"Jermain, come take a look at this," she said.

"What is it?"

"Come over here."

Jermain paused his video game and groaned as he made his way over to the couch and saw the pus coming out of a massive ulcer on Cas' back.

"Draw his blood the old way and feed it to Father,"

Jermain told her, his voice blazing with rage. "We might lose him soon."

VOYAGE NIGHT 21

The Mummy played on the small television. It seemed to be playing on a loop. Cas' head was turned toward the screen, his mind trapped in a nightmare, forced to stare at the same movie, repeatedly. The mixture of Nex and marijuana only made things grimmer. He lay quietly on the couch, his eyes open, sweat beads lining his face, his mind stuck in a hellish vortex of Egyptian imagery.

"Try to enjoy it," Jazzie said softly. "It hurts when you fight it." She was referring to the Nex she'd given him, a dose more than enough to kill a bear.

Am I going to die? The thought echoed in Cas' mind. *I can't move. Why can't I move?*

A jarring growl rumbled from Jazzie's throat, tickling his ear, and Cas saw her fangs.

Vampires! Everything makes sense now. Their cold hands; only seeing them at night. I should have known! Casimir's eyes struggled to stay open. *What a fool I've been!*

Jazzie's fangs sank deep into Cas' neck, her lips cold and firm against his skin. Jazzie drained his blood, leaving him pale and weak, his eyes glazed over as he lost consciousness.

———

Colette sucked Cas' neck hard, filling her mouth with a generous amount, then made her way over to her father. Standing over the front panel of the coffin, she opened her father's mouth and served him the blood, like a mother bat feeding her pup milk.

She and Jermain stood hovering over their father, staring with hope that something would happen—yearning for him to wake. Charles laid motionless as the blood he had been fed leaked out of the side of his mouth. He gurgled it back out the way it came in. His body seemed to reject it.

"I don't understand. Why isn't it doing anything?" Jermain said, shaking his head sadly.

"Home," Cas garbled.

They turned around and looked at Cas, who was back on his feet, now stumbling around, teetering like a drunken top.

Colette went over to him and set him back on the couch. Drops of blood glissaded from the bite wounds in his neck.

"No-no-no! You're going to hurt yourself. You stay right here," she said, then kissed his forehead.

He didn't fight her. The drug had made him pliant. He curled back up on the couch, his head wilted onto the pillow, and in another moment, he nodded off.

"You rest now, baby," she said.

"Stop calling him baby. What are you two, an item or something?" Jermain said, scowling.

"I'll call him whatever I want!"

———

A few hours later, Cas began to tremble violently. His face turned a sickly purple.

"Cas! What's the matter?" Colette asked. She slapped his face lightly. "What's happening?" Her eyes widened.

"Our saint is overdosing. You gave him too much Nex. Drained him of too much blood," Jermain said. "Goddamnit. You don't know when to stop, do you?"

Jermain went into the medicine bag and pulled out an ampule of naloxone and a syringe. Wasting no time, he hurried over to Cas and plunged the syringe straight into his arm. After a few seconds, Cas stopped convulsing and went limp, his forehead still sweaty, his skin clammy, resembling someone who had been accidentally locked in a sauna for several hours.

"He should be all right in a few hours," Jermain said. He put down the syringe and returned to his chair. His shoulders were hunched, and he stared down at the floor. Colette thought her brother's sadness and defeat could be felt all across the Atlantic.

She remained seated near Cas and caressed his face softly. "You're going to be all right. You'll be well again," she said.

Jermain glanced over at their father. His head rested peacefully inside the coffin's pillow top. He looked even more shriveled and sickly compared to the beginning of their voyage, Jermain thought. *Something went wrong. Why didn't Casimir's blood work on Father?*

"We're going to get to Denmark in two days and Father still hasn't woken up. That son of a bitch Alexandru lied to us. We should've seen a change by now!" Jermain stood up, his fists clenched tightly, and punched the wall with all his vampire might. The blow formed an enormous crater in the wall, triple the size of his fist. He punched again with his left. The impact echoed violently; a booming quake shook the metallic container.

"Stop it! Stop it!" Colette cried. "You'll punch through!"

Jermain continued to smash and pound the wall with his fists, the bone on metal clamoring and ringing in all directions. Jermain glanced at Colette, who had brought her hands to her ears and appeared to be sobbing.

Then, suddenly, a blinding red light radiated from Charles' coffin. Jermain blinked rapidly. Through the nebulous light, he saw his father sitting upright, eyes opened wide. Still shaking from hitting the container wall, Jermain found it difficult to catch his breath. *Am I dreaming? Is that really Dad, awake?*

What happened next left Jermain both stunned and horrified. Their father levitated from his coffin and hovered, suspended several feet in the air. Charles' arms were crossed, and his body rotated upright and remained suspended in mid-air above their heads. Their father's skin glowed a healthy complexion (compared to how he'd looked for years), and his bone mass had filled out. No longer appearing weak, his eyes looked alert and sharp. They were cobalt blue and appeared to be full of energy. Charles was completely transformed before their eyes.

"Father," Colette gasped. Jermain could feel her shaking beside him.

"Father! How do you feel?" Jermain asked.

"Exuberant, my children. The blood you've given me has invigorated my spirit." Charles' voice blared through the container. Jermain noticed Casimir stir and readjust himself on the couch. Father's voice must've woken him out of his stupor. Cas shifted his frail body like a listless zombie on the small couch.

Charles' gaze shifted toward Casimir. "This little lamb has the most succulent blood I've ever tasted." He hovered over toward Cas, sat him upright, and stared at him closely, the way a predator might examine its prey before devouring it. "Why does his blood taste so good?"

"He's what you needed, Father," Jermain said in a shaky

voice. "We searched far and long to find him. We're glad he's served you well." He glanced at his sister, whose eyes welled with red tears. "We're so happy you're feeling well again."

"My beautiful children. How I've missed seeing your faces and conversing with you both." Charles looked down at his limbs. He seemed to be appraising how his arms, legs, and torso had filled out and looked healthy again.

Jermain looked on, thinking that their father's strength had been rejuvenated. Charles' eyes sparkled, just the way he remembered them from when he was a young boy.

"I've been in an endless sleep, haven't I? I feel so much more...*alive*," he said, snarling toward Casimir.

Charles turned and sank his sharp fangs deep into Cas's neck, digging violently, carving new holes in his tender skin. Blood sprayed in all directions.

"Father, be careful not to drink too—" Colette attempted to pull her father from Cas. Charles smacked her arm away.

"Don't you dare tell me what I can and can't do!" Charles shouted.

She cowered.

"I haven't felt this good in such a long time." As he spoke, globules of blood leaked from his mouth. His voice carried a bass that shook Jermain, sucking out all his toughness and bravado until he felt like a small child again.

Jermain remained quiet as he watched his father suck more of Casimir's blood the rest of the evening and into the morning. Charles only stopped to take breaks to speak to them about the tastiness of Casimir's blood and all the blood they would drink when they'd arrive in Russia. Jermain wanted to tell his father to pace himself—tell him that he'd had enough. They already knew they had their limits. Too much human blood could be fatal. Who knew what too much of a saint's blood would do?

Charles Dupré praised Jermain for concocting what he described was an ingenious plan to escape the States and migrate to Russia. Once they arrived, he said, they'd be safe to live as they pleased without the threat of being hunted by American authorities.

Colette remained several feet away from her father, looking fearful. Jermain thought Charles would be more loving toward them when he was finally cured. Unfortunately, the newfound power and vigor quickly inflated his ego, leading him to indulge in excess without regard for any consequences. His behavior, Jermain thought, reminded him of a Roman emperor with a God complex.

CHAPTER 14

HANG TIGHT

DETECTIVE FLYNN CARESSED his beard and mustache, which had been growing out sloppily over the past week. He knew he looked disheveled, not having bathed or gone home for three days. Officer Diaz didn't hold back. She told him how badly he smelled. He barely took his wife's phone calls. Behaving in this way was a sure way to get served divorce papers at the office, but he didn't care. He was going to get to the bottom of this case and find those kidnappers. He picked up his desk phone dialed out.

"Agent Peters," someone on the other end answered.

"This is Detective Patrick Flynn from the NYPD calling. I've been in touch with you on the portal."

"What's the case number, please?"

Detective Flynn provided the agent with the number.

"Got it. We have a team working on it now, Detective. Someone will reach out once we have an update. Hang tight."

Flynn didn't leave his desk for the next thirty-six hours.

He remained logged into the Portal, checking it anxiously every few minutes, only taking breaks to go to the bathroom. He'd considered peeing in a 7-11 cup but his inner voice scolded him and told him he should avoid it at all costs and maintain some decency. Mainly in an effort to be considerate toward the women and rookies in the office.

Diaz brought him dinner later that night. After that, he ate protein bars he'd stashed away in his desk, and he sent rookies to grab him coffee from the deli down the street.

He waited and waited for an update. At three thirty-seven the next morning, Flynn received the following message on the portal:

```
INTERPOL case number: 2802048
Missing person alert for: Casimir
Jaworski
Age: 17
Nationality: USA
Location: North Atlantic Ocean
(Latitude: 57.689194; Longitude:
9.506305)
Notes: Ship is near Copenhagen,
Denmark. Fugitive identities are
unknown.
```

Flynn sighed, pressing his fingertips to his temples. Now that INTERPOL had a lead, it was only a matter of time before they'd locate and arrest the abductors. He thought about their location—a cargo ship bound for Denmark—and the questions that plagued him. Why did they abduct Casimir? Why didn't they just kill him like Rick and the others? The criminals' nebulous actions perplexed Flynn, but the case was beyond his scope now. He had to bury the case file in his mind. The investigation was no longer his to pursue. *Something's definitely rotten in Denmark,* he thought. *Very, very rotten.* It was up to INTERPOL and Danish authorities to do their due diligence and find those bastards.

CHAPTER 15

VOYAGE NIGHT 23

THE CARGO SHIP docked in the Port of Copenhagen twenty-three days after it had left the Port of Newark.

On the eve of the twenty-second day of the voyage, Charles began to get sick from drinking too much of Casimir's blood. At first, he began to regurgitate the blood. Then the violent seizures began. His head and body trembled wildly, and despite what Colette and her brother did to alleviate his pain, his condition worsened.

On the twenty-third day, Charles let out a chilling wail that shook his children's bones. When they went to check on him, a dark, odious fluid had leaked from his nose and mouth. He convulsed a few times before he lay completely still. The shine he had exhibited shortly after drinking Casimir's blood had vanished. Colette and Jermain tried to awaken their father for two hours straight, until they realized there was nothing they could do. He was dead.

Then, almost as if seeing through a looking glass in a terrible dream, Colette watched as their father's body dried up and disintegrated in seconds. She stared inside the coffin at what remained—a pile of dark gray ash.

All go to one place; all come from dust, and all return to dust, she thought.

The rage that overtook Jermain for the next half hour startled her to her core. She sat on the floor, crying red tears, as Jermain smashed everything inside the cargo container to bits. He tore the chest freezer from the floor and heaved it to the end of the container. It opened in mid-air and all the food and blood bags spilled in all directions. Colette didn't attempt to stop him for fear that in his rage, he'd strike her. She sat near Casimir, shielding him protectively, fearful that Jermain would kill him. After a while, though, she realized Jermain didn't seem to want to harm Casimir. He did, however, dig his long, sharp nails into his own wrists and tear flesh from his chest. Colette looked on in shock and silent horror as Jermain wrenched at his beautiful blonde hair and tore it all out.

"Why go on?" Jermain asked.

She'd never seen him look so broken.

"What's the point?" he whimpered, as blood flowed from his self-inflicted wounds.

Rivulets of blood flowed from Colette's eyes. All she could do in that moment was sit near Casimir and cry. She hoped her presence would deter Jermain from harming him. She'd decided she would interject if he tried to harm Cas. But Jermain's rage was directed at inanimate objects and himself; he didn't put his hands on either of them.

When she'd gathered more energy, she begged: "Stop, Jermain. Please stop."

He didn't seem to hear her. He appeared deaf to every noise, every utterance outside of his fury. The only sounds Jermain seemed to be hearing were the sounds of ignoble failure and loss. A sadness consumed her with a magnitude she didn't think was ever possible.

Colette knew Casimir's IV drip had run out two days ago, and he hadn't eaten anything solid for over three days. She wanted to take him with them. She really wanted to. But Jermain wouldn't allow it.

He's as good as dead, Jermain muttered, as they were evacuating the container.

He'd been doing something near their father's coffin, but she was too distracted and in too much shock to really notice what.

"Au revoir, Casimir," Colette said, as she kissed him gently on his forehead before leaving the cargo container.

As she slipped out onto the ship and followed behind her brother, the cool breeze tasted salty and wet with the freshness of the ocean. She was tired of crying and forced herself to stop, knowing she'd need her energy for their escape.

CHAPTER 16

PORCELAIN SKIN

AT APPROXIMATELY FOUR fifty in the morning, the Port of Copenhagen's dock swarmed with Danish police vehicles.

Henrik Larsen, an INTERPOL agent, led the way onto the cargo ship. Larsen was followed by twenty-two other agents and officers. With help from the captain's assistant, they located the shipping container where a crew member had reportedly heard loud noises. He described a violent rattling and a tumultuous banging that began around three in the morning and lasted for about half an hour. When the crew member approached the container, he swore he'd seen it shake and even heard yelling from within. Something that could make a container move the way it did was worth reporting, the crew member said, glancing around fearfully, still shaken from the incident.

As Larsen and the law enforcement agents approached the container, they noticed the door was slightly ajar. He held a flashlight, peering in, and moved slowly through the large opening. A putrescent smell immediately upset him.

He jerked back and held his arm across his face in a futile yet instinctual attempt to block the reek of decay and rot.

"What is it?" an agent behind him asked.

"Terrible smell," Larsen answered.

He took a deep breath and regained his composure. He continued forward, followed by several agents carrying semi-automatic weapons and flashlights. The flashlight beams probed the container's contents.

It looked as though a hurricane had whipped through it, ravaging the items inside into metal shrapnel and plastic debris.

"I think I see a coffin!" one of the agents cried out.

"Freeze! Don't move!" Agent Larsen said, as a blanket on the couch stirred.

The agents directed their flashlights toward the couch, revealing a pair of pale legs.

"Don't move! If you attempt anything we'll open fire!" Larsen yelled.

He and four other agents moved toward the couch. There was blood everywhere. They noticed a bucket filled with vomit and excrement near the base of the couch.

Larsen felt tense as he approached. He took a quick, deep breath, allowing his finger to be close to his gun's trigger in case he needed to use it.

Slowly, carefully, he reached out. His heart raced. Larsen removed the blanket. The agents' flashlight beams revealed a young man—a teenager—whose skin glistened in the light like porcelain. The beams crossed up and down the boy's body. Upon further inspection, Larsen saw dark, swollen, black and purple discolorations all across his thin frame. As they moved their flashlights up toward his head, they stopped at his neck, where several deep intrusions appeared. Small streams of blood trickled from the wounds.

It looked like he had been stabbed in the neck with a two-pronged carving fork several times. The young man's eyes were closed, and he lay in a damp layer of sweat and blood.

Larsen pressed his index and middle finger against the boy's neck. "We need medical care!" he shouted into his two-way radio. "I feel a pulse. He's still alive!"

SHORTLY AFTER CHARLES DUPRÉ dissolved into ashes, and after Jermain went mad and destroyed the inside of the cargo container, he and Colette carefully disembarked from the ship. They abandoned Casimir against Colette's wishes, as Jermain considered him dead weight. He argued that since their father was dead, Cas was no longer of any use to them and would only slow them down. Colette protested but realized the noise Jermain had made while smashing the wall may have been heard by the crew, and it was only a matter of time before the authorities showed up. Before they left, Jermain scooped up what he could of his father's ashes and sealed them in a heavy-duty, water-resistant container.

Jermain led them to the far end of the dock, away from the parking lot and loading areas. He scanned the dark ocean and seemed to be in deep thought about what to do next.

"How are we going to get to Russia?" Colette asked.

"We'll figure it out later. We need to find shelter soon, before the sun comes up."

Colette understood the urgency and got moving.

Running from the police for over one hundred years had given them a sixth sense—an intuition—that authorities were nearby. Both of them had sensed it and knew they didn't have much time. It was time to flee.

"There are islands all around us," Jermain said, pointing toward the water. "There aren't many people on them, and we can hide out there for at least the day until we figure out our next move."

"How will we get there?"

"We'll have to walk underneath the water. It's too deep to swim or tread across. Make sure not to take in any water. You won't be able to walk after if you do."

Colette groaned and said, "I'll follow you."

They dove off the dock and walked underwater for two kilometers—for about thirty minutes—until they reached land. Colette followed behind him. He turned every now and then to make sure she was still there.

———

The small island they landed upon was Trekroner Fort. Colette glimpsed a sign that welcomed tourists.

As she climbed up the jagged rocks, she noticed several large wind turbines, their sentinel blades jutting out of the water, approximately fifty, sixty feet from where she stood. She gawked at the enormous power-generating structures as they rotated macabrely, whirring in the early morning twilight. A cool breeze lapped her face. The gigantic wind turbines reminded her of the old windmills she'd seen years ago around Louisiana, when she was a young vampire. These were ten times taller and much more modern. In that moment, she felt like an anachronism. The world had been passing her and her family by, and she hadn't even realized it. Her surroundings now felt foreign; alien. She felt out of place, always running, always hiding. She hated her life now more than ever, especially now that they'd lost their father. Her depression was deep and gloomy, like the early morning Danish sky.

"We'll hide here until tomorrow evening, then I can look at ship schedules," Jermain said. "We should still follow our plan and go to Russia."

Colette folded over and threw up on the grass. "I hate the taste of salt water," she said, heaving violently.

"You aren't supposed to swallow it," Jermain said, shaking his head.

"I didn't mean to," she cried, wiping the muck off her mouth with the back of her hand. "It's hard not to." She hunched over with her hands on her knees, unsure if she'd be sick again. She looked up at Jermain. "Why'd you save Father's ashes?"

Jermain held the container with one hand, observing it under the moon's silver gleam. She could feel the sun beginning to creep over the horizon and knew they'd have to take shelter soon.

He shrugged. "It seemed like the right thing to do."

"He's dead, though..." Her eyes remained fixed on the container. "Right?"

"Do you remember what Alexandru said?"

"Oh, god, Jermain." Colette threw her hands in the air. "Not him again. I don't want to hear about—"

"Hear me out! He said it's really hard to kill a vampire." Jermain held the clear container up high as the dawn light began to hit it. For one second, it seemed as though the ashes flickered. "We are proof of that, sis. I think we can bring Father back. Somehow."

Colette's brow furrowed and her eyes narrowed. "I've

been doing everything you've told me to do for over one hundred years. I've followed your directions wholeheartedly—" she let out a tired cry. "But, I'm sorry. Dad is dead, and you've lost your fucking mind! Why didn't you want to bring Cas if you still think we can bring Dad back? Why'd you leave him?"

There was a long silence. Jermain didn't answer her and kept his gaze fixed on the container.

For the first time in her undead lifetime, Colette thought about ending her life. How would she do it? People had been trying to kill her for over one hundred and fifty years, and so far, they'd been unsuccessful. They'd hurt her for a few days or a couple weeks if she was weak, but she always managed to bounce back. Her father had died so easily, she thought. After all they'd done for him and all they'd been through, his life had ended with such ease. Yet, she and Jermain were still roaming the earth. They were strong and growing more powerful, it seemed, like some sort of Ancient Gods, wandering amongst mortals.

"How do you think you could bring him back?" Colette asked, attempting to avoid another blowup argument.

"I think Şerban might still be alive. So, if we're able to bring Father back..." he held the ashes up to the moon light, "and we can find Şerban to get him to feed Father his blood—"

"Jermain! Do you hear yourself? Our father is dead. You're holding his ashes! Do you even hear yourself right now? Have you lost your goddamn mind?" Colette clutched her hair with both hands. "We need to figure out a way to get away from here so they don't find us and kill us. That's it. Forget about Father. We can grieve once we're somewhere safe. But, right now, we're wanted and they're coming for us."

Searchlights suddenly appeared in the darkness. A police helicopter materialized over the horizon; its searchlights cut brightly onto the nearby water. Colette and Jermain sprang behind a brick wall, just in time to avoid being exposed.

"Cole, you have to have faith. We have a gift," he said, pressing his back against the wall. "There's magic inside of us. Don't ever forget that."

"Let's just find a place to sleep for the day. I'm tired," Colette protested. They'd been through so much in such a short amount of time, and daylight was upon them. Daylight meant certain death, so they had to act quickly. In another few minutes, their bodies would burst into flames.

"There," Jermain said, pointing toward an opening in one of the forts. He pulled his sister along, and they entered darkness.

Remembering she had a waterproof lighter, Colette fished it out from her pocket, flicked the flint wheel, and illuminated the stairs.

They skipped down a spiral staircase.

After a few moments, they arrived at an underground cellar that was well out of the sun's reach. A crypt-like bunker lay before them, laden and fortified with concrete. She spotted sepulchers that were large enough for them to lay in.

"Jermain," Colette said, as she nestled into a sepulcher.

"Yeah?" he said, crawling into another.

Colette glanced over at him, dimly illuminated by the faint lighter. She watched her brother as he adjusted himself, making himself comfortable.

"Wherever we go, there we are—the basement dwellers."

Jermain laughed for the first time in his undead lifetime.

"That's true, isn't it?" He clutched the container filled with their father's ashes tightly, protectively.

Colette put her lighter away and all was masked in darkness. She stroked her necklace, a ritual she practiced to make sure it was still with her before she went to bed. Her lucky necklace, which Uncle Lucien had gifted her.

As she closed her eyes, she heard her brother say, "And there we are."

CHAPTER 18

BISPEBJERG HOSPITAL

AS SOON AS Patricia Jaworski received word that Casimir had been found and was hospitalized in Copenhagen, she purchased a one-way ticket to Denmark. She didn't sleep the entire eight-hour flight, the trip a sleepless haze. Her nerves were the worst they'd ever been. Even compared to when she'd lost her husband, the police visit, and the realization her son was kidnapped, she now experienced another level of physical pain; an intense stress that made her entire body ache.

She arrived at Copenhagen Airport and hailed a taxi to Bispebjerg Hospital, where Casimir had been admitted. The six-hour time difference, the long flight, and her nerve-wracking anxiety made her question how she continued to function. Her body moved like a somnambulant, processing each movement as needed, her sole objective aimed at reaching her son.

When she arrived at Cas' room, she encountered a policewoman guarding the door. After showing the officer her identification, she was allowed to enter.

The nurse was called in and informed Patricia that

Casimir was still in a coma. When she first laid eyes on him, her tears welled, and the floodgates lifted. Her son had lost anywhere between forty and fifty pounds. Already thin to begin with, now he was emaciated. *What have these people done to him?*

The nurse brought over a chair for her to sit on and handed her a box of tissues.

Patricia sat down slowly. She ran her hand across his forehead and felt his cold, damp skin. It was hard to believe he was still alive. If not for the EKG machine's fluttering electrical waves, confirming his heart still beat, she wouldn't have believed it. Dark circles lined his eyes. He was as immobile as a rock. She could hardly tell this person laying on the hospital bed was her son.

The officer approached Patricia. "When your son wakes up, we're going to have to ask him some questions."

Patricia dried her eyes with a tissue, then blew her nose. "Is he in a lot of trouble?"

"In the United States, he may be. But the authorities here weren't able to locate his kidnappers. They fled the scene. Perhaps he can help us with our investigation."

Patricia felt like she'd aged ten years in just a few weeks. She hadn't eaten anything in over twenty-four hours. The policewoman must have noticed and gently put a hand on her shoulder.

"Would you like something to eat? I can ask the staff to bring you something if you'd like," the officer said. "Or, if you need a break, there is a cafeteria on the second floor."

"No, thank you. I'm not hungry." She couldn't take her eyes off her son. *When will he wake up?* She turned toward the nurse. "How long does someone stay in a coma for? Usually?"

The nurse glanced at Casimir. A feeding tube had been

lodged in his mouth, taped so it wouldn't fall out, and wires crisscrossed all over his head and body.

"It's difficult to say...it depends on the severity of his injuries," the nurse answered, in a tone that let Patricia know they were doing all they could.

"Mrs. Jaworski—" the officer began.

"Yes?" Patricia whispered. She was on the verge of crying all over again.

"I understand you've been through a lot," the officer said, "but, did you know the people who kidnapped your son?"

"I only met Jazzie once. She didn't seem like a bad person...when I met her."

"She went by Jazzie? That's not her real name, is it? Must be a nickname. The American authorities weren't able to match it to any real identity."

"Christ," Patricia said. "I don't understand how my son got mixed up in all this? He's a good boy. I tried to do everything in my power to lead him in the right direction." She hunched in the chair and covered her face with her hands. "Where did I go wrong?" She didn't want her question answered. The feeling of defeat consumed her as she bawled, hunched over, her hands over her face.

———

Casimir woke up from his coma two months after he was found by authorities in the cargo container in the Port of Copenhagen. The doctors said it was a miracle he'd lived. He was dehydrated, malnourished, and had severe pressure ulcers all over his back and rear end. Small scars covered his frail body. The mysterious puncture wounds, looking like they were made with a narrow ice pick, had greatly alarmed the doctors and medical staff.

His mother stayed by his side every day, waiting for him to regain consciousness. An elderly woman had rented her a spare bedroom at an affordable rate. It was about a fifteen-minute walk to the hospital, but she slept most nights at his bedside, only using the rental to bathe and clean up sparingly.

The police kept surveillance on Casimir night and day. They attempted to question him as soon as they noticed he was awake, but he refused to speak to them for several days, even though he could. He tried hard to remember the events that had transpired. He wanted to get his story straight before potentially incriminating himself. But he couldn't remember a single thing. When he was told he was found inside a shipping container on a cargo ship, nearly half-dead, he was speechless. They'd shown him photographs from the scene in an attempt to rekindle his memory. Nothing. He couldn't believe the story he was told. The police explained to him that Jazzie, Seth, and their father had kidnapped him in New York City and were planning to take him to Russia.

All he could recall was the night he had kissed Jazzie. It was a memory he cherished and was glad he still had it, but he couldn't remember when exactly that had happened, or anything beyond that moment.

Casimir watched the physiotherapist closely as she moved her fingers in an arced motion, touching each fingertip to her thumb in turn, one at a time.

"Now you try," she said.

Propped upright in the hospital bed, Cas attempted to

copy her movements, but he fumbled. His hands seemed clumsy. He sighed and looked down at them in defeat.

"It's all right. Your range of motion will improve in time. Be patient, Casimir... How are you feeling?"

"Confused. I can't remember anything."

"Are you in any kind of pain?"

"No."

"What's the last thing you do remember?"

"I remember kissing Jazzie. But then her brother showed up."

"Was that when they kidnapped you?"

He stared up at the ceiling and took a deep breath. "I don't remember anything about that. This was back in Queens. I don't think that's when they kidnapped me. Everything's still so...foggy."

"I understand," she said. "You've been through so much. The psychologist will be in shortly. You may not think you are, Casimir, but you are improving." She patted his hands. "We'll work on moving those toes a bit during our next session. Try to rest and not stress yourself out. I'll see you tomorrow."

It had been two weeks since Casimir had come out of his coma, but his mind was still lost in a gloom. He had difficulty concentrating and grew tired easily, finding physical therapy to be extremely challenging despite taking frequent breaks. He overheard his mother speaking to the doctor one morning, expressing her concern about the state of his brain, since he had virtually no recollection of his kidnapping.

Later that afternoon, after his session with the psychologist, his mother brought him a cellular telephone.

"Someone wants to speak to you," she said, handing it to him.

"Hello?" Cas asked.

"I've been worried about you, man. Everyone's been worried!"

"Andrew! How's it going?" He was excited to hear a familiar voice. Cas smiled up at his mom, and she returned the smile.

"I'm doing all right. How the hell are you? You're famous. You're all over the papers here," Andrew said.

Cas laughed softly. "Really? There've been a few reporters snooping around outside my room, trying to come in to ask me questions, but the police get rid of them every time they come by."

"How's your recovery coming along? Are you feeling better?"

"I'm getting there. My memory—" He paused for a moment and he examined his fingers dully, attempting an exercise movement the physiotherapist had taught him.

"It's all right, man," Andrew cut in. "You've been through a lot. I'm glad you still remember me." He chuckled. "I'm sure it'll come back to you. I just wanted to say a quick hello. Your mom told me you're still not feeling that great so I should probably let you rest. Listen, first thing you do when you get back is come over to my place. We'll order some pizza and fire up my Volcano. Thing is sick, dude!"

Cas laughed.

"Miss ya, bud," Andrew said.

"I miss you too, man. I'll definitely let you know when I'm back home. They have me doing physiotherapy and all sorts of other stuff. I'm just taking it one day at a time, you know?"

"Absolutely, man. Little by little, you'll get back to your

old self. Give me a ring anytime you want to talk. Your mom has my number."

"All right, dude. I'll talk to you soon. Thanks for the call."

"Get better soon. Later, man."

Cas hung up the phone. He felt a relief of pressure. It was nice hearing from his best pal. He wanted to get back home, but he knew it would take time. He wasn't ready to leave the hospital just yet.

He then wondered what had happened to Jazzie and Seth. He'd heard they were still on the run, having fled the cargo container just before the police and INTERPOL had arrived, and they hadn't been caught yet. Did they end up going to Russia? That's what the authorities said their plan had been—to take Casimir to Russia and disappear. A mix of excitement and wonder engrossed his thoughts. *Why didn't they kill me? They easily could have. I'm sure the police and the authorities were asking themselves the same questions. Maybe they thought I was dead and left me behind. I guess I'm lucky to still be alive. I should be grateful.*

CHAPTER 19

VLAD DRACUL

PÉCS, HUNGARY 1475

THE HOUSE WAS DIMLY LIT and cool. Alexandru entered Vlad's blood-red chamber with a forceful stride.

"They have arrived," Alexandru said vehemently.

"Bring them in," Vlad replied.

Alexandru turned into the corridor and in a moment, he returned with three elderly women trailing behind him. They marched into Vlad's cavernous bedroom. Candles lined the sills and recessed shelves, illuminating the red walls of the room.

He saw Vlad studying the women who entered. They were very old and they all wore long black dresses, black embroidered blouses, and all three donned headscarves. Their gold necklaces, gaudy earrings, and filigree jewelry chimed as they shuffled into the bedroom.

Turning toward Alexandru, Vlad asked, "Where is your brother?"

"He's still in Curtea de Argeș but he will join us soon," Alexandru said.

Vlad nodded in agreement.

"Maestru (master)," the women called out in unison as their eyes met Vlad's.

Vlad's eyes gleamed at the sound of their praise. He had been feeling inferior for a time, since he no longer resided at Bran castle, having been ousted and dethroned due to his long imprisonment. The word *master* was a refreshing boost for his ego.

But it didn't matter that he was no longer living in the castle. He would reassemble and when the time was right, he'd retake his throne one day soon. The man was bred a warrior and there were still plenty of disciples who followed him—who had sworn their eternal allegiance towards him. There were many who had served with him during war and many who would serve with him again. Those true disciples, the ones who would follow him until his last day, moved to Pécs to be near him when they'd heard of his release from prison. His followers professed he emanated an aura, a power, which they could feel when they were near him. They claimed they'd been deprived of that power while he was away.

"Sorceresses," Vlad said.

"We are happy that you've been released from prison." The women in black bowed at his feet. "Our lands, our people have missed your presence," she hissed and then the three women chanted something unintelligibly in unison. "We are here to serve you, master." Their voices rang loudly. Their chanting was a throng of execrations, a litany of maledictions.

"Please. I've been away a long time. My powers have left me. Let us begin, sorceresses," Vlad said.

"As you wish, Master. We are here to serve you," one of the women said. Her eyes had no pupils. They were all sclera and, in a blink, the white eyeballs were eclipsed with a black film.

The sorceress spread a tapestry across the middle of the oak floor. A large design—a coat of arms—a crescent moon above a six-pointed star with six horizontal stripes, covered the center of the tapestry. One of the women positioned a medium sized iron footed cauldron on top of the silk spread. Vlad began to take off his clothes. Another sorceress who carried an alchemy bag took out a half ounce gold bar and dropped it into the cauldron. She waved her hand over the cauldron and the gold began to melt. Smoke rose out from the blazing cauldron as the gold sizzled. She waved her hands in a necromantic motion, manipulating the gold without touching it.

"We are ready to begin. Bring out our sacrifice."

Alexandru marched to another room where a girl began to wail, and, along with two guards, dragged her out. She was a beautiful, young Vlach girl, who wriggled and fought the guards, desperate to get free. Her legs flailed and scraped against the hard wooden floor, but she was powerless. The guards pulled her towards the sorceresses.

The sorceress' chanting grew louder and more frantic as the girl was taken to the small altar they'd assembled. One of the witches took out a long, sharp knife and held it up to the young girl's neck as a guard ripped off her chemise, revealing her naked body. The men held her upright in their grasp, facing the altar and the women who stood there. Her limbs seemed to give way, either through exhaustion or sheer terror, and she drew in deep, heavy breaths as she looked away from the witches, her eyes searching the room as if praying for someone—a miracle—to arrive and rescue her, pluck her out of this wicked scene.

"No! Please" The words burst from her lips. "Please, I

don't want to die." Her voice broke as she struggled against the hold of her captors, frantic, desperate. "Please, I beg you."

The witch slashed at the young woman, leaving bright red streaks across her breasts. She screamed once as blood sprayed from her body. Another of the sorceresses maneuvered the cauldron under the young woman and caught her blood as their chants grew louder.

"Dark God, hear our prayers. We've brought a lamb to sacrifice. Hear our prayer! Bless Lord Dracul with vigor and energy. Feed him life with this blood."

A howling wind ripped through the room, swinging open the wooden sashes on the windows. The sorcerers' headscarves were blown back and Vlad's chaotic long, black hair lashed in the gale. The sorceress gripped the blade and sliced the girl's body, cutting at her thighs, arms, and face. Red blood flowed from the girl's once-smooth skin, now ripped to shreds.

The third sorceress held a thick grimoire, the pages were open to tiny text and symbols, her index finger pointed at their victim. She chanted verses in an unknown tongue, while the second sorceress captured all the blood she could, as if she were a participant in a perverted game. The young woman's blood mixed with the molten gold.

"Bea (drink)." The sorceress holding the cauldron motioned towards Vlad.

Vlad dipped his cup into the cauldron, taking a large swig of the hot liquid. Red gold dried on his mouth and dribbled down his chin, forming a pasty crust.

The sorceress with the alchemy bag took out a prong and a casting tool and began to bang at the gold mixed with blood. After several minutes, she held up a necklace of bizarre quality and design. She placed it over Vlad's head.

As it settled on his neck, it seared him, sizzling and fusing into his skin, a painful process. Over his moaning, the scent of roasting flesh filled the air. The gold gave off a dull, reddish-orange hue—the incongruous mixture of human blood and gold.

"This necklace will give you power, my lord. It will bring you strength as well as protect you during battle," the sorceress said, laying a hand on his forehead to quiet his writhing, stilling his body.

Vlad released a long, ragged breath and drank more from the cauldron, then passed it to Alexandru.

"Drink, my brother," Vlad said, his voice hoarse. "Drink to long life."

ACKNOWLEDGMENTS

Many people aided me in this book's development. Frankie Lopera and Katja Douedari made particularly large contributions to the process. I would also like to thank Younes and Barbara, Ana Elisa Zoia, and Joe David Melendez.

A special thank you goes out to my Kickstarter backers, who supported me very early on. Thanks to Juan Elias Lopera for being my very first beta reader.

Thanks to my editors, who worked very hard throughout the writing process and helped flesh out the story.

Lastly, a huge thank you to my amazing cover designer, Sandeep Karunakaran (Sanskarans). You truly inspire me to keep creating.

They have my eternal gratitude.